SON
OF
MFUMU

·····································

A CHANGA'S SAFARI ADVENTURE

MLTON J DAVIS

MVmedia, LLC
Fayetteville, GA

Copyright © 2018 by MVmedia, LLC.

All rights reserved. No part of this publication may be roduced, distributed or transmitted in any form or by any means, includingotocopying, recording, or other electronic or mechanical methods, withohe prior written permission of the publisher, except in the case of brief dations embodied in critical reviews and certain other noncommercial uses mitted by copyright law. For permission requests, write to the publisher, dressed "Attention: Permissions Coordinator," at the address below.

MVmedia, LLC
PO Box 1465
Fayetteville, GA 30214
www.mvmediaatl.com

Publisher's Note: This is a work of fiction. Names, aaracters, places, and incidents are a product of the author's imagination. Loales and public names are sometimes used for atmospheric purposes. Any resemblance to actual people, living or dead, or to businesses, companies, events, institutions, or locales is completely coincidental.

Book Layout ©2017 BookDesignTemplates.com

Ordering Information:
Quantity sales. Special discounts are available on quantity purchases by corporations, associations, and others. For details, contact the "Special Sales Department" at the address above.

Son of Mfumu/ Milton J Davis. -- 1st ed.
ISBN 978-0-9992789-0-1

Contents

To Pop. Finally finished.

The worst you can do to a man is break his name.

—Swahili proverb

- 1 -

The feeble flame pricked the thick blackness, a fruitless effort against an overpowering void. A man sat before the anemic fire, his muscled upper body bare except for the intricate tattoos etched into his umber skin. A leather loincloth draped over his waist, resting on his thick crossed legs. His face was unknown; a wooden mask concealed the features. He swayed to a rhythm unheard, his breathing in time with his side to side motion. To one observing he seemed in a trance. But such was not the case.

The foliage about him trembled but the motion and sound did not break his state. Three shapes entered the faint light; beings resembling the mysterious primates inhabiting the densely forested hills. One look into their hard faces and gleaming eyes revealed a different presence.

The Ndoki sat side by side opposite the swaying man, their eyes locked on him. The man swayed for a few more moments then ceased.

"What have you seen, Usenge?" they asked in unison.

Usenge, the masked sorcerer, ruler of the Kongo, peered at his cohorts through the eye slits of his permanent mask.

"The son of Mfumu has returned," he said. His voice was deep and ancient like the river meandering near them.

"What of the tebos?" they asked.

"They have failed," Usenge said.

"Then it was meant to be."

Usenge nodded.

The Ndoki stood together. "Will you be ready?"

Usenge stood before his masters. "I will."

The Ndoki disappeared into the bush. Usenge eyes lingered where they once stood. They would not help him as they did with Mfumu. He was alone in this fight. He shrugged his shoulders. It did not matter. He was much stronger now. He would not fail. Changa Diop would die.

He stomped the fire with his bare foot, extinguishing the flame. The darkness rushed upon him like a lover long denied and he took comfort in its embrace.

The wrecked dhow lay on the desolate beach, rocking with the coming and going of the waves. The midday sun heaped its light and heat upon it, salt water mist rising from the broken wooden planks like formless sprites. Within the broken dhow's small hold Changa Diop sweated as he rustled about, gathering everything he could carry while cursing and praising the ancestors in a single breath. For weeks it seemed Oya held him within her hands, blessing him with steady winds which sped him along the coast. He landed when necessary to replenish his supplies then continued south, following a mental map passed on from merchant to merchant for millennia. So far that oral map held true.

But as the distance between Changa and Yoruba-land increased it seemed Oya's attention waned. The storms he saw in the distance passed closer and closer, churning the waters and forcing Changa to take more care to his sails. Then the storm that beached him fell upon him in full fury, challenging every ounce of Changa's strength and skill. The howling wind seemed to curse his name, the lightning falling around him like arrows. The storms pushed him closer and closer to the shore despite Changa's best efforts. He was eventually able to steer the small dhow to a shoreline clear of rocks, or at least he thought so. The stone he struck lurked just below the surface, pouncing like a predator then gashing his hull. He managed to reach the shore before sinking.

He was sure this was Usenge's doing. The sorcerer was powerful and now that Changa was closer to his lair it made sense that his attacks would increase in intensity and frequency. Changa carried his provisions to the shore, and then arranged them on the sand in order of importance. He absently played with the talisman hanging about his neck, symbols of his previous journeys and the people who accompanied him on those adventures, people who he now knew as family. There was the Orthodox cross given to him Mikaili, a parting gift when his old friend gave up the sea to finally fulfill his dream of becoming a priest in his homeland of Ethiopia. Panya's amber necklace hugged his neck, the stones warm on his skin. Zakee's jambiya pressed against his waist, tucked into his sash. And then there was Warani's bracelet circling his wrist, his formerly silent companion he'd known as the Tuareg. If they had their way each of them would be beside him; at least everyone except Panya and young Zakee. Sadness touched him as he remembered the Yemeni amir, his exuberance, his energetic storytelling and his bravery. It was his death that made him realized how much he cared for his crew. Panya was the only person who had the opportunity to come with him. It was she who explained to him how important it was for him to go alone. Usenge was not the only demon from his past he had to face.

The storm had forced him to sail beyond his destination. He was stranded in the Namib, the massive desert which ran along the coast for miles. How far he'd missed his mark would determine how arduous his journey would be so Changa took no chances. The beach quickly climbed into towering dunes, which would force him to travel close to the shore. After securing his provisions he set out north.

As he trudged through the thick sand, Changa sensed he was being observed. He glanced upward to the dunes. Something moved, dipping out of his view. He looked away, peering from the corner of his eye. The figure reappeared, pacing back and forth along the cliff's edge. Something was definitely following him. What or who he could not discern. Changa shifted his direction, walking parallel to the barren heights instead of toward them. As he proceeded his attention was pulled away by barking sounds and a strong smell of animal waste. He saw movement ahead of him, a dark mass writhing atop the sand. As he came closer the mass separated into familiar shapes. Changa had encountered a massive herd of seals. The local waters were abundance with fish and the waterborne mammals had chosen this beach as a mating ground. Changa veered away from the shore, hoping to avoid the mass. As he skirted the animals he caught movement from the corner of his eye again, but now it was coming toward him. Changa dropped his gear, snatching his kashkara free in his right hand, a throwing knife in his left. A group of male simbas charged from the dunes, led by a massive male whose mane billowed with the sea wind. Changa recognized the foulness in the creature's eyes and a smirk came to his face.

"You have found me Usenge," he said.

The smaller simbas surged by the tebo simba. Changa spun then ran as fast as he could toward the seal herd, hoping to throw off the simbas. The sea beasts bellowed warnings then undulated toward the surf, but their efforts were much slower than Changa's. Whatever command the tebo held over the felines was usurped by the opportunity to feed. They fell upon the seals, ignoring Changa as he sprinted through the throng. The tebo was not distracted. Changa was its prey. It tracked Changa with its misshaped eyes, running parallel with him. Changa knew he could not outrun the monster; he would have to confront it as always. He stopped running then strode toward the beast with throwing knife and sword. The tebo reared on its hind legs then roared before dropping to all fours and bounding toward Changa. Changa took a wide stance, waiting for the right moment. When the tebo was only a few strides away he threw the knife with all his might. The blade spun to its mark, striking the tebo between its burning eyes. The beast's momentum was so great it continued toward Changa, who fell flat as the beast careened over him. Changa rolled onto his back then scrambled to his feet as the tebo flailed about, clawing at the blade. Changa threw another knife, this one lodging in the tebo's neck. To his surprise the beast continued struggling. It was stronger than the tebos he'd encountered before. With only one knife remaining, Changa did the only thing he could do; he ran.

He was almost to the top of the dunes when he heard the unnatural roar of the tebo. The beast had pulled the blades free and was pursuing him at full speed. He crested the dunes to what he hoped he wouldn't see; a barren stretch of sand with no sign of any hiding place. There was nothing left for him to do other than turn around and wait.

The tebo exploded over the dune rim like a strange bird of prey. It leaped the distance between it and Changa, its roar filling Changa's ears. Changa stood still, waiting until the tebo almost upon him, its mouth gaped wide. As the beast wrapped its forelimbs around Changa's torso he drove his sword into the roof of its mouth then withdrew his hand, his forearm sliced as it slid across the tebo's fangs. The tebo's mouth locked, held open by Changa's sword. Changa ignored the claws digging into his back as he stabbed the tebo's neck with his last remaining throwing knife, the only weapon that could kill the beast. The tebo howled and its gripped tightened. Changa drove the knife deeper and deeper. Why wouldn't it die? Was it because of the nearness to its creator? Changa could do nothing but continue stabbing. He was trapped in the tebo's grip.

The beast howled again, but not from Changa's efforts. It thrashed its head from side to side then with a sudden effort threw Changa away. Changa landed hard on the hot sand, the wind knocked from his lungs. He gasped until his breath returned then grimaced at the pain emanating from his back. Turning to his side then lifting up on his elbow he watched the tebo twisting from side to side, surrounded by bare-chested brown men in loincloths wielding long iron-tipped spears. They attacked the tebo with coordinated precision, plunging their spears into its body then backing away before it could retaliate. To Changa's surprise the tebo slowly succumbed to their attack, slumping into the sand then letting loose one last howl before dying. Changa shuddered as cold spread from his back wound, slicing through his body like an invisible knife and taking his energy with it. The hunters who had slain the beast were running to him as he blacked out.

He awoke to a canopy of glittering stars. A fire crackled nearby, the aroma of charred meat reaching his nose and sparking his empty stomach to grumble. He felt wetness against his back and immediately sat up, fearing the worst. He reached back and felt some type of poultice covering the wounds inflicted by the tebo. Looking toward the flickering light, he spotted the warriors that had slain his adversary sitting cross-legged around the fire speaking in a language he could not decipher. Each held a stick with a portion of meat on the end over the flame. One of the hunters looked in his direction then spoke loudly. The others looked toward him, the smiles gone from their faces. The hunter who saw him first stood, walking to him with his stick. He squatted before Changa, offering him the meat. Changa took it then ate it, the warm succulent morsel pulling a moan from his dry lips. As Changa chewed the man walked behind him to look at his wounds. He spoke, but Changa did not understand. Changa knew Arabic and Kiswahili would not serve him here, so he reached back into his memory for a language he had not spoken since he was eight years old.

"Thank you for saving me," he said.

The man's eyes brightened and he nodded.

"You are BaKongo?" he asked.

Changa nodded. "Yes, though I have been gone for a very long time."

"We are Khwe," the man said. "What is your name?"

"Changa Diop," Changa replied.

"I am Shasa," the hunter said. "Why was the spirit beast trying to kill you?"

Changa grinned. "I have a powerful enemy in Kongo."

"A sorcerer?" Shasa asked.

Changa nodded. "They follow me wherever I go. Only I have been able to kill them with my knife."

Shasa extended his hand and Changa gave him the throwing knife. The Khwe closed his eyes then hummed as he ran his hand across the blade. He opened his eyes then handed the blade back to Changa.

"The smith who forged this knife possessed powerful nyama," Shasa said.

"The smith was my baba," Changa replied. For the first time in many years a memory flashed in his mind, one not of that terrible day when Usenge murdered his baba. He was very young, and he watched his father practicing with his knives, the blades that would one day belong to him.

"He was a kabaka then," Shasa said.

Changa's eyes widened. "Yes, he was. You are very perceptive."

"You are very open," Shasa said.

The Khwe stood. "Come join us at the fire. You are a long way from home but we will take you there. We know the way."

Changa stood, taking a moment to steady. He was still weak yet strong enough for travel.

"Thank you," he said.

Shasa folded his arms across his chest. "Are you sure you want to return?"

"I must," Changa replied.

Shasa smiled. "Yes, you must."

He joined the Khwe at their meager fire. They were seven total, three men, three women and one child on the brink of womanhood. Shasa introduced him to the others and they continued their meal, sharing a single gourd of water. After the meal they slept, resting from the ordeal of the day. Changa slept better than he had in many nights, comforted by being in company of others. Once again, he found himself thinking of his former crew; the mysterious Tuareg, irascible Mikaili, young and curious Zakee, and Panya. His mind lingered on Panya and he smiled as he recalled her beautiful face. Why it took him so long to love her puzzled him but at the same time agreed with him. Theirs was a love that took time to develop, which made it as strong as a baobab. If he did not return from this safari, at least he knew he had loved a woman like no other.

Changa and the Khwe set out for Kongo the next morning. Changa fell into their ways, keeping the pace and helping with the hunting and foraging the best he could. Nothing escaped their gaze, from the smallest insect to the largest tembo. Yes, there were tembo in the Namib to Changa's surprise. The lumbering behemoths he knew required much water to exist, but these creatures had adapted to their surrounding as most creatures do when challenged by harsh lands. It was the tembos that led them to rare caches of water where they replenished their supply. Changa learned that there was little in the desert the Khwe did not eat. Despite his distaste he did so as well, knowing that he had to stay nourished. Changa's years as a merchant trained him to be a quick study of different tongues. He quickly picked up many of the words and phrases of the Khwe and sang their songs as best he could. As his rudimentary vocabulary improved the others took to him, explaining their ways and asking him questions about his life before encountering them. Soon he was the storyteller before the fire, explaining with words and gestures his travels and adventures.

The small band lounged under the sparse shade of a solitary acacia, resting from a recent hunt. As was usual Changa was the center of attention

"Why did you leave Kongo?" Shasa asked.

"I didn't want to," Changa replied. "The sorcerer, Usenge, killed my baba and was planning to kill me, too. I was taken away by my elders to safety and to train for the day I would avenge my baba's death. But Usenge found me and attacked the village where I hid. I escaped alone, and that's where my journey began."

"But you took so long to return," Shasa said.

Changa nodded. "You have heard my stories. I hoped to become wealthy enough to raise an army to defeat Usenge and kill him. Yet her I sit alone among you without a single gold coin or one companion."

"It is best this way," Shasa said. "If you had come with an army, your people would have seen you no different that this Usenge. Now you must win their trust and convince them to follow you."

"I suppose you are right," Changa said.

"I am right," Shasa replied. "I always am."

Shasa grinned as the others laughed.

Weeks passed and the desert ebbed away, re-placed by grasslands and shrubs. Apprehension grew inside Changa, they were edging closer to the Kongo. After another week the forest wall loomed before the band. The Khwe gathered around Changa, pressing talisman into his hands and hanging them around his neck as they hugged him. Shasa was the last to approach.

"Are you sure this is what you want?" Shasa asked.

"It is not what I want," Changa replied. "It is what I must do."

"Then I hope you fair well, Changa of the Kongo," Shasa said. "Know that the Khwe are your friends."

Shasa tied a bracelet made of twisted wood around his wrist.

"It will guard you against the tebo," Shasa said

"Thank you," Changa said. He reached into his bag then took out a jade necklace.

"This was given to me by an emperor of the Middle Kingdom," Changa said. "In some lands it is worth a fortune. Today, it is a gift to a friend."

Shasa took the necklace then hung it about his neck.

"Goodbye, my brother," Shasa said.

Changa swept his gaze over the people who had become his companions.

"Goodbye," he said.

Changa took a deep breath, and then strode toward his homeland.

-2-

Usenge brooded over the simmering iron pot, his breath hissing through the nose and mouth slits of his mask. A cloak of woven tree bark fell from his broad shoulders, teasing the back of his muscles thighs and thick calves. A tangle of talisman necklaces hanging from his neck swayed across his bare chest. The sorcerer stared into the brew, awaiting the message he knew would come. The tebo had been the most powerful sent thus far yet still it failed. If not for the interference of the desert folk Changa would be a pile of dry bones in the Namib.

The enchanted concoction rippled suddenly as if a stone had been tossed into it. Usenge leaned closer to the conjure pot. The voices that rose to his ears were heavy with anger.

"You cannot avoid that which has been foreshadowed."

"I am not avoiding anything," Usenge replied. "I am hastening the inevitable."

"You waste our strength. Be patient; he will come to you."

"So, I am to wait for the usurper to appear within our midst before destroying him? Best kill him now."

"He possesses nyama we must have. It is obvious to us now. It is beyond that of a kabaka. It is a strength we have not seen before. It is a strength that we desire."

The Ndoki's words revealed what he had suspected all along.

"You have conspired against me!" Usenge
shouted. "Am I not enough? Am I to be pushed aside by
you like I was by Mfumu?"

There was an unnerving silence before the Ndoki
responded.

*"You are what we have allowed you to be. Do not
forget this. We embraced you when your own rejected
you. We shared the secrets of the Deep Forest with you
despite your weakness. You are strong because of us.
What we do beyond your presence is not your concern.
You have what you desired. We will insure that you will
keep it. Do not waste our time or strength on your
schemes. Wait for him."*

Usenge could not deny the wisdom of his masters. Everything they said was true. Still, he was not going to be deterred so easily.

"I am your servant," Usenge said. He placed the
lid on the noxious brew before touching his head to the
ground in respect to those who had given him the power
to hold the position he now possessed. Twenty-five years
ago, he wandered into the bush a bitter man, angry that
Mfumu had been chosen to be kabaka. He wandered too
far; entering woods that were forbidden to the baKonga
because of those who dwelt there. He remembered well
the day the Ndoki came to claim him and he shuddered.
What he thought would be his death became his blessing.
Instead of consuming him, the Ndoki claimed him, sharing their secrets with him and initiating him into their
own. Unlike them he did not yet wear the *mokumbusu*
sheath. Usenge possessed the body of a warrior, broad
shouldered with a muscled torso and thick powerful legs.
Only his face showed his mark, he wore the carved

14

mask, the talisman of the Ndoki, the conduit of nyama linking him to his brethren.

A warrior entered his house and quickly prostrated before him.

"Kabaka, he has come," the man said.

"I will meet him soon," Usenge replied.

The warrior crawled backward from the house. Usenge stood then grabbed his staff. As he exited his guards fell into step behind him, each carried a short spear, a sword strapped to their waist and dagger strapped to their forearm. They moved stiffly, their eyes unblinking, their mouths slightly open. They were Tukuju, half-dead warriors who had once defied Usenge and now served him. The staff in his hand controlled them; they did not eat or sleep and fought with a fury far beyond any living man. The fear of them alone kept most at bay; those who had attempted to take his life became one of them.

Usenge strode to his stool which rested before a blazing fire, his entourage quickly prostrating before him. His visitors honored him in their own way, removing their hats and bowing deeply. Their leader, a man with straight black hair and a pink face covered with hair, stepped forward and bowed again. He spoke the Kongo language with an accent that amused Usenge.

"Great Usenge, thank you for allowing this humble servant to be in your presence once again," he said.

"Welcome back, Joham," Usenge said, his perfect pronunciation of the pale man's native tongue causing a few of his new crewmembers to look at Usenge in wonderment.

"I see you have brought more men from your homeland," he said. "I find this disturbing."

Joham's smile quickly faded. He knew well not to anger Usenge.

"Forgive me, Great Usenge," Joham said. "I had to replace those who were lost during my last visit. The sicknesses of your land take a heavy toll. I also needed them to deliver your gifts."

Usenge felt a rush of interest.

"You brought them?"

Joham's smile returned. "Yes, as you commanded."

"Show me," Usenge ordered.

Joham turned to his men then nodded. They separated to either side, revealing the cannons. Usenge stood then swiped his arm. Everyone moved further away, including the Portuguese. Only Joham remained beside the weapons.

Usenge circled the cannons, inspecting them with eager eyes. He heard of their destructiveness from the coastal tribes when these men who called themselves Portuguese first encountered his realm. The Portuguese used them to establish a beach head, blasting the villages into oblivion from the decks of their ships. The villagers had come to him for help and Usenge responded. His warriors waited until the Portuguese had moved inland beyond the range of their cannons then slaughtered them. The weapons they carried, arquebus, were loud yet useless against his Tukuju, but the cannons showed promise.

Joham trailed behind Usenge, his face twisted in expectation.

"They are fine weapons," he said. "The best money could buy."

"I'm sure they are, for you would know better to cheat me, Joham. You wouldn't want end up among my Tukuju."

Joham swallowed. "No, I would not. However, there is the matter of payment. Such perfection is not free."

16

"Nor should it be," Usenge answered. "You will receive half your gold now, the rest when you have completed our agreement."

"Will that include slaves?" Joham asked.

"If you do as I asked you will have all the slaves you need," Usenge replied. "All that you do not kill belong to you."

Usenge returned to his stool. The Ndoki ordered him not to attack Changa and he would obey them. Changa's relatives were another matter. Until now he had let them be, leaving them to fight among themselves for a title that would never be theirs. Word of Changa's return could possibly unite them. That would not matter, but Usenge did not need the distraction, and the planning of their demise would give him something to do as he waited for Changa's arrival. His musing was interrupted when the rude Portuguese cleared his throat.

"Great Usenge, may I inquire about the whereabouts of this enemy you wish to be subdued?

Usenge studied the man before answering. Joham claimed that Portugal was a great land ruled by a man he called Dom Joao the Second. Though they possessed interesting items, Usenge found the Portuguese standing before him weak and easy to manipulate. The coastal people had accepted them readily, taking on their religion and assuming their names. These were people Usenge had driven from his land and terrorized; they were seeking protection from his wrath and assumed these pale people from across the seas would do so. They were wrong. After Changa was destroyed he would send ambassadors to Portugal to determine whether he should make it part of his realm. From what he had seen so far, it was not worth the effort.

"Kandimba!"

A masked warrior broke from the ranks then prostrated before Usenge. Kandimba was as tall as the sorcerer with a body hardened from war. He wore the commander's war mask, a symbol of Usenge's favor.

"My life is yours!" he shouted.

Usenge nodded then turned his attention back to Joham.

"Kandimba will lead you to their villages. Once you have defeated them you can claim them and all that is theirs, except their leader. He belongs to me."

"And the gold?" Joham asked.

"Do this and you shall have all the gold you desire, more than you can imagine."

Joham eyes glittered with Usenge's words. Greed was a sickness among these people, which made them easy to manipulate but also easy to turn. He did not trust Joham and the others, for their loyalty was as deep as their money pouches. But for now, they would serve a purpose.

"Leave me," Usenge said.

The Portuguese took a deep bow then returned to his ranks. Kandimba stood, waiting for additional orders.

"Learn to use the cannons," Usenge said in their native tongue, speaking too fast for Joham to follow. "If the Portuguese fail kill them all."

"I think we should kill them either way," Kandimba replied.

"Not yet," Usenge said. "We may have use for them in the future. Make sure you bring Muhongo back to me. He will make a fine Tukuju."

Usenge gave Kandimba the staff that controlled the Tukuju.

"I will not fail you," Kandimba said.

"I know you won't. Now go."

Kandimba turned then strode to the Portuguese as he raised his spear. His warriors surrounded him; together they led the Portuguese and their cannons from Usenge's presence, followed by the Tukuju.

Usenge smiled through his mask. The end had begun.

- 3 -

Changa trudged down the narrow path, frustration clear on his face. For days after he'd separated from the Khwe he'd walked his former home and encountered no one. His shallow memory from childhood was failing him. Although he remembered the language he once spoke, he'd lost familiarity of the land where he once lived. But he was only eight when he was forced to flee his home. As a boy he saw very little of his father's domain, and as he fled for his life he noticed little else. It could be that he was in a region he'd never visited.

Still he figured he should have come across some sign of life by now. It was as if the people were hiding from something or someone. There were moments when he felt he was being watched, yet his observations and senses revealed nothing except troops of ill-tempered monkeys. He traveled until noon, the sun high and hot overhead. His meal consisted of dried meat from a kill days ago and fruit picked from a tree he recognized from his youth. As he chewed on the tasteless meat he caught the sound of a voice. Changa sprang to his feet, frustration replaced by hope.

A person came into view, a man covered with bark-cloth clothing and wearing a wide straw hat. He walked hunched over, supporting himself with a tall staff. The man mumbled, his free hand waving as if fanning away a bothersome insect. Changa cleared his throat to get the man's attention but the man kept walking toward him at a fast pace, oblivious to his effort.

"Excuse me uncle," Changa said aloud.

The man stopped immediately, his head jerking up. He squinted at Changa with eyes capped by gray eyebrows. A gray moustache twisted with his lips, matching the scraggly gray beard growing on his chin and neck.

"Uncle, can you see me?" Changa asked.

"Of course, I can see you!" the man shouted. "I see everything. I have the eyes of a hawk and the soul of a demon! I see here and beyond. Even a ghost like you does not escape my scrutiny!"

Changa was puzzled. "Ghost? Uncle I am not a ghost. I am a man just as you."

"Really?" the wizened man tipped up to Changa.

"What is your name, man like me?" he asked.

"I am Changa Diop," Changa said.

"Aha!" the man exclaimed, pointing an accusing finger at Changa.

"Changa Diop is dead! He died soon after Usenge stole his father's stool."

The fact that the man knew him gave Changa hope. The old man shuffled around him, inspecting him from head to toe.

"You are the ghost of Mfumu! Yes, that's who you are."

The old man's eyes widened.

"Yes! Yes! Mfumu! The ancestors have finally heard us! Mfumu has returned to free us from Usenge!"

The old man turned then ran away, moving much faster that Changa imagined he could.

"Wait!" Changa yelled. "Wait!"

The man kept running, waving his hand and staff over his head.

"Mfumu has returned! Mfumu has returned!"

The old man took a sharp turn then plunged into the thick bush. Changa ran after him, his pursuit hampered by vines and trees so thick they gave no hint of what awaited beyond. Roots battered his feet and he was forced to climb over fallen tree trunks. The old man moved through the forest with ease. For a moment Changa was puzzled but as he watched the old man fade into the distance he saw a pattern in his flight. This wasn't a random run through the forest; the man followed a path he knew well. Changa mirrored the man's movements, deftly avoiding some of the obstacles that had slowed him earlier. It was good that he did, for some were traps meant to maim or kill. He barely avoided a shallow pit filled with wooden spikes most likely drenched in poison, and he took the time to walk around a log whose surface was riddled with tiny blades. He looked for the old man then saw his escape became more direct. They had apparently evaded the hidden gauntlet and were near the old man's destination.

The murmur of a large settlement came to Changa's ears. The vegetation quickly cleared, revealing a tight yet well-traveled trail. The familiar smell of an urban site came to him as well, especially the aroma of cooking food. The odor opened memories in his mind, days of watching cooks before large simmering pots prepare his family's food as his mother and sisters talked and laughed. The emotions stirred reminded him of the most important reason he had come home; to free them from Usenge's grip. There was nothing he could do for his father, but he could rescue his family.

The trees thinned and Changa could finally see the city. It was much larger than he imagined, vibrant with men, women and children going about their daily chores. The city was ringed by fields tended by the women and children, while in the distance Changa spied the men tending herds of small cattle and goats. The people watched the old man as he ran down the now wide road to the main city, some calling at him and laughing. They fell silent as Changa emerged into the clearing. Some stopped their work to stare; others grabbed their children and fled toward the city as well, yelling as they ran. People gathered at the city's edge as he came closer; not soon afterwards the warriors appeared. Some brandished short swords and spears, others aimed small bows with poison arrows. Changa stopped outside of what he estimated was bow range then raised arms to his side, his hands spread wide. He would not fight these people no matter how they approached him.

The old man broke through the throng followed by a contingent of warriors. Each were powerfully built and walked in a way that conveyed their experience. The tallest of the group walked with the old man, a skeptical look on his face. His body was lean and tightly muscled, indicating a man who was experienced in fighting. They halted a few feet away from Changa; the tall man approached him, looking him up and down.

"See, Enyama!" the old man said. "It is the ghost of Mfumu!"

"I see no ghost Kaihemba," Enyama said. "I see a man who has tricked you to find our city. I say he was sent by Usenge."

The mention of Usenge's name stirred anger in Changa. As he lowered his hands the warriors raised their weapons.

"It was he who told me who I am," Changa replied. "But I am not Mfumu. I am his son."

The warrior laughed. "I know you lie now, Tukuju. Changa Diop is dead."

The warrior lunged at Changa with his short sword. Changa twisted to his right and the sword missed its mark. He reached for his Damascus but stopped. If he killed this man it would take him longer to convince the others, if he could persuade them at all. Instead he decided to rely on other skills, those he learned long ago in the fighting pits of Mogadishu.

The warrior attempted to back swing with his sword but Changa caught his wrist and then twisted it behind the man's back. He shoved him into the charging warriors, a few of them crashing into him and falling. A warrior who managed to avoid the tangle lunged at Changa with his spear, grazing his cheek. Changa grabbed the spear shaft, yanked it from the man's grip then spun it about, striking him on the temple. The man fell to the ground unconscious.

The warriors recovered. They regrouped before Changa, some grimacing from their wounds. Changa tossed the spear aside and prepared for the next assault. The warriors looked at each other as if considering who should attack first. Changa smirked then winked at the old man.

Enyama finally stepped forward.

"You don't fight like a Tukuju," he said.

"I don't know what a Tukuju is, but I suspect it is another one of Usenge's monsters," Changa answered.

The warrior eased his stance as did the others.

"I believe you don't serve the Usurper, but I don't believe you are Changa Diop."

"What do you know, Enyama?" Kaihemba said. "I thought you knew how to fight until now."

Enyama glared at Kiahemba then shoved him away.

"Shut up, Kiahemba!" Enyama turned his attention back to Changa.

"The old man is crazy but he does speak the truth…sometimes."

Kiahemba looked insulted. "Sometimes? Sometimes?! Changa, beat him up again! The ancestors demand it!"

"There will be no more fighting," Enyama said. "Come. I will take you to our kabaka. After you meet with him we will decide what to do next."

"I thank you for the honor," Changa said. "But can I eat first? I'm famished."

Enyama smiled. "Yes. I know just the person to fill you up."

Changa followed Enyama, Kiahemba and the others into the city. The gazes he received ranged from friendly to suspicious as they passed through the compounds. They finally entered a compound near the city center, an area usually reserved for major families and the kabaka. The compound vibrated with activity; women and men going about the business of the day and children playing under the watchful eyes of their family. The activity came to a halt as they entered, all eyes falling on Changa. Enyama walked up to the women gathered around the well. He approached a heavy-set woman, her arms folded across her ample chest. She did not seem happy to see Enyama, let alone Changa.

"Greetings, Maikulu."

"What do you want, Enyama?" she asked. Her tone confirmed her mood.

"This man claims to be Changa Diop, Kabaka Mfumu's son. He's hungry."

The woman laughed, and the other women joined her.

"Then he is a ghost," she answered.

"See! I told you," Kiahemba exclaimed. "The ghost of Mfumu!"

"Shut up, Kiahemba," the woman said. "Come, I have some food for your stranger."

They followed the woman to her compound. In the middle of her hut was a boiling concoction of stew tended by two girls. Their cheerful smiles greeting their mother faded when they saw the others.

"It's okay," Maikulu said to them. "They are my friends."

Maikulu gestured for Changa to sit as she prepared a bowl for him. The stew was delicious and he ate it voraciously.

"So, who are you really?" Enyama asked.

"I am as the old man said," Changa replied. "I am Changa Diop."

The others looked at each other, skepticism still on their faces.

"Why would you come back?" the woman asked.

"To free us, Maikulu, that's why," Kaihemba said. "I have seen it. The ancestors have shown me."

"There was a time I thought that was my task," Changa said. "I imagined myself leading a large army to fight Usenge for my home. But here I am alone. I have one goal; to kill Usenge and free my mother and sisters."

When Changa looked up from his bowl Enyama and Maikulu looked at him with astonishment. Kaihemba looked at him with satisfaction.

"See? What did I tell you?" Kaihemba said. "He is the son of Mfumu. What outsider would know of Mfumu's family still being held captive by the Usurper?"

A wave of relief swept over Changa.

"They are still alive. That is good."

"We will take you to the Elders," Enyama said. "You may have come here alone Changa Diop, but you will have your army."

Changa placed his bowl down. "What are you talking about?"

"We have waited a long time for your return," Enyama said. "As you can see, many of us had lost hope. But first we must visit the Elders and send out the word."

Enyama jumped to his feet. "I'll gather the warriors. Maikulu, can you gather the others and prepare our supplies?"

"Of course, Enyama."

Changa felt their optimism. All the years of travel and preparation were finally bearing fruit. Panya was right, he left his homeland alone and he had to return alone to gain the trust of his people. His travels were never about building an army; they were about him becoming physically and mentally ready to confront Usenge and avenge his father's death. He was ready.

When Changa looked up Maikulu was still sitting before the stew pot.

"We will gather provisions, but you will go nowhere today," she announced. Her eyes fell on Enyama. "This man needs rest."

"What are you talking about?" Enyama said. "We must leave to see the Elders immediately."

"No. He will stay the night."

The voice uttering those words caused Enyama to stiffen and close his eyes. Changa turned to the speaker, a man almost as tall as Enyama but stouter in appearance. The wrinkles teasing the corners of his eyes and the gray scattered in his hair signified him as an elder. He swept the room with a disapproving stare before his eyes met Changa's. His expression changed when he looked upon Changa and a smile came to his face.

"If you had brought him to me when you came to the village I could have told you who he was," the man said. "I knew Mfumu, and if I didn't know better I would think I was gazing upon him once again," he said.

"I am sorry, *sekula*," Enyama said. "I did not wish to burden you with this issue."

"I know what you wished, Enyama," the man said. There was a moment of quiet tension between them before the elder spoke again.

"Welcome to our village Changa Diop," the man said. "I am Lusati."

Changa bowed his head to the elder. "You must forgive me if I do not recognize you. I was very young when my father died and he knew many people."

"Even if you were a man at that time you would not have recognized me," Lusati said. "I was a young warrior then. I served your father, but I'm sure he did not know me. He was a great man. I was there the day Usenge took his life. There was terrible nyama at work."

The image of his father's death flashed in Changa's head and a snarl came to his face.

"I apologize if my words disturbed you," Lusati said.

"Don't," Changa replied. "I have carried that pain with me since that day and will carry it the rest of my life. I have come to avenge him and free my family, though I doubt doing these things will ease what I feel."

"Those are wise words," Lusati replied. "Come, you will stay at my compound tonight. Since Maikulu has taken it upon herself to serve you she will serve us tonight."

"It will be my honor *sekula*," the woman replied.

"Enyama will join us as well."

Enyama forced a smile to his face.

"Yes, sekula," he answered.

"And what of me?" Kaihemba said. "It was I who brought him here! If it wasn't for me he'd still be a wandering ghost claiming to be the son of a kabaka!"

"You may come as well, Kaihemba. But we will not suffer any of your ranting."

"I only repeat what the ancestors tell me," Kaihemba fussed. "And the ancestors have a lot to say!"

The group walked to Lusati's compound. The residence occupied the center of the village, the houses surrounded by a wooden wall. A large ancestor tree rose from the center of the compound, its expansive branches offering shade to those below. As they entered, Lusati's family surrounded him and followed him to the tree. A stool surrounded by gris-gris rested against the base. Lusati took a seat and was immediately flanked by his bodyguards and family elders. Changa sat before him, Kaihemba and Enyama beside him.

"After your father died I and the others warriors fled to the bush," Lusati said. "The months after his death were terrible. We fought Usenge with all our might, but his nyama was too great. The Ndoki emerged from their forests to help him, conjuring all types of monsters to break us. Many of us became monsters as well."

"The Tukuju," Enyama said.

"What are they?" Changa asked.

"They are his bodyguards and his servants," Lusati replied. "And many of them used to be our family."

"He claims the bodies of those he has killed them brings them back to life," Kiahemba explained.

"They are the core of his army," Enyama added. "They are not skilled fighters, but they do not have to be. Unlike us, they cannot die."

"I am very familiar with Usenge's creatures," Changa replied. "They have haunted me most of my life. These Tukuju are new to me."

"And yet you still live," Lusati said.

"Usenge sends his tebos for me," Changa said. The mention of the words made the crowd groan in unison.

"Do not call those demons among us!" Kaihemba said.

Lusati looked at the old man sideways.

"It has been a long time since the tebos have stalked our land," he said. "Usenge considers us defeated, although he may think different now that you are here."

"Where have you been all this time?" Enyama asked. "How did you survive?"

"For many years I wandered the bush alone," Changa answered. "Every time I tried to settle the tebos would find me. As I grew older I fell in with the Wandering Tribes."

Lusati frowned as Changa uttered those words. His village had probably been victims of nomads at one time or another, as had most cities and villages on the edges of the realm. Those were the preferred targets, people who could not protect themselves and were far enough away from the central powers to receive aid. Changa was not proud of those years; he was a much different person then, a boy growing into a man in a world that offered him nothing but hate, harshness and fear. The death of his father haunted him frequently then and he did almost anything to ease the dregs of terror left behind.

"I did what I had to do to survive," Changa said. "The Wandering Tribes were the only people that would take me in. When I discovered why I didn't care. They were vicious and cruel yet I felt safe among them. As long I did what I was told I was protected."

"You were a boy," Maikulu said. "No one can fault you for your choices. You did not know."

Her sympathetic smile eased his guilt.

"I didn't," Changa agreed. "My time with the Tribes came to an abrupt end when I was a young man. We angered a powerful kabaka who managed to unite the local tribes into one large army. They tracked us down then attacked, killing most of us. I was captured and sold into slavery. I served as a pit fighter in Mogadishu until I was freed by a Swahili man named Belay. I served as his bodyguard for a time then eventually became his protégé. He taught me the merchant trade. When he died he left me his trade and his dhows."

A smile had returned to Lusati's face.

"We know the Swahili," he said. "They bring items to trade for ivory and other goods. They are good people, at least those we have met so far. *Safiri macho wazi ili uwe msomi.*"

Lusati's fluent Swahili brought a smile to Changa's face.

"That is what they say," he replied. "Yet I feel I am still learning."

Food was served and Changa ate heartily again, still famished from his long trek. Afterwards he shared more of his safari, capturing his listeners' attention with details of such far off lands as the Middle Kingdom, Vajyanagar, Songhai and the Oyo cities. By the time the fire became embers he was full and exhausted.

"We will rest tonight," Lusati announced. "Tomorrow I will send out runners to contact the other cities. We'll gather to see what the Elders have to say."

He shared a proud smile with Changa.

"Everything you have done has led this moment. The ancestors have forged you into the man you must be to face Usenge. Once we meet with the others and confirm your return we will gather our warriors and go on the march. It is time to end Usenge's terror once and for all."

A smile came to Changa's face as well.

"Yes it is," he replied.

- 4 -

Joham and his soldiers marched behind the baKongo warriors through the thick bush, their armor and weapons a painful burden. He sometimes questioned his decision to ally himself with Usenge, for it resulted in him performing challenging tasks such as the one before him which distracted him from his true purpose. Still, it had brought rewards, and this expedition could prove to be the most lucrative of all. The gold and ivory he'd been paid previously had been most welcomed and useful, but it was slaves he was after. Portuguese nobles were willing to pay a high price for the servants of this land and Joham was more than willing to provide them. He'd formed a strong bond with the leader and would use it to his advantage as long as he could.

The nervousness he experienced came from the lies he'd told to gain Usenge's trust. He was no more the representative of Portugal's Dom as a spider was the child of a fly. Joham was merely a soldier of fortune as was the men who followed him, a man who deserted the ranks of the Dom's army to pursue wealth his own way. His cohorts were a collection of rivals, men of soiled reputations from England, the Levant, France, and Spain. He forged the letters he'd presented to Usenge as his proof of contact with the Portuguese king. If Usenge knew, he had yet to let on.

The cannons they dragged through the bush had been salvaged from an abandoned shipwreck he had been lucky enough to find on his way to the Azores. The men he picked up at various ports with the promise of more gold than they could imagine. So far Usenge had allowed him to fulfill that promise, which turned out to be double-edged sword. Once their pockets were full they disappeared at the first landing, most never to return. Very few were as far thinking as Joham. Every voyage to him was an investment, an opportunity to establish something far greater that slave trading and treasure hunting.

His musing was interrupted by the Spaniard. Alfonso de Caderroa claimed to be a blue-blood noble but his behavior indicated just the opposite. He claimed his family was one of the great houses fighting against the Moors in Granada, yet he quickly volunteered to join Joham on his voyage. He insisted that they bring a priest with them to convert any pagans they encountered on their journey to the true faith but Joham wanted none of that trouble. Usenge would kill them all the moment anyone challenged him; it was best to leave that discussions for those with grander schemes and larger armies.

"How much longer must we march through this tangle?" Alfonso asked.

"As long as we need to," Joham replied. "We have a task to perform."

"We have enough gold to last us years," Alfonso replied. "The hell with slaves."

Joham cut a mean eye at Alfonso.

"This is my expedition. I am in charge. The gold that weighs you down is there because of me. When you purchase your ship, gather your crew, sail through storms praying for God and nails to hold it together and form your alliances with your kabaka, you can do as you please. For now, you'll do as I say."

"No need to be so angry," Alfonso said. "It's just that there are places where our gold will buy us all we need for much less effort."

"And you know of these places?"

"I have heard of them."

"I have heard that there is land where men and women live forever and walk about naked in the eyes of all that is Holy," Joham said. "But until I see this land, it doesn't exist."

Alfonso frowned. "You are not a dreamer, my friend."

"This is dream enough," Joham replied.

Kandimba's sharp voice called out and the ba-Kongo warriors halted. Joham raised his hand and his men did the same. Kandimba marched up to Joham, his hard eyes staring through his war mask.

"Come with me," he said.

Joham followed the warrior ahead, Alfonso trailing behind. They trekked to the edge of the bush. Just beyond the trees was an expanse of grass and shrubs leading to a solitary steep tree covered hill. Smoke rose from the summit, a clear indication of a village or city. Kandimba pointed at the hill.

"That is Cilombo," he said. "It used to be the stronghold of Changa's uncle, Ngonga. Changa took refuge there after his father's death. It was meant to be a stronghold, but Usenge sent the tebos and they destroyed it. It lay dormant for many years until Ndonga's son Caungula returned and re-established it."

"So why doesn't he send these tebos to destroy it again?" Alfonso asked.

Kandimba turned to look upon the outsiders.

"Why should he? He has you and your cannons. If you wish to claim slaves, they are at the top of this hill. Just make sure you don't kill them all first."

Alfonso folded his arms across his chest.

"So, we are to risk our lives for this..."

"Be quiet, Alfonso," Joham said. "Go back to the men. Now."

Alfonso glared at Joham before marching away.

"You should kill that one," Kandimba said. "His tongue will cause you much trouble."

"You may be right," Joham replied. "But not yet. But Alfonso has a point. We can't get our cannons close enough without them seeing us."

"That is no worry," Kandimba said. "They will not attack. They do not need to. Cilombo is a fortress. They will wait for us to attack them. The hillsides are filled with traps and the road leading to the summit is a maze. They do not know of your cannons. They won't know until it is too late."

Joham studied the hill for a moment longer, rubbing his bearded chin. The cannon would give a huge advantage, but Joham was not one to be overly optimistic.

"We will need a distraction just in case they decide to attack," he finally said.

"I will send Tukuju up the hill," Kandimba replied as if expecting Joham's decision. "The traps mean nothing to them. They will only slow them down. But if you wish to claim any slaves you must subdue Cilombo before the Tukuju reach the top. If you don't, you will not gain any."

"Many of the Tukuju will die," Joham said.

Kandimba grinned. "They have died before."

A chill raced down Joham's spine.

"We will move the cannons into position tonight," he said.

"That will be difficult," Kandimba commented.

"But necessary," Joham replied.

"It seems we have a plan then."

"Yes, we do," Joham said. "What will you and your warriors do?"

"We will wait and watch," Kandimba said. "If the attack does not go as planned, we will act."

Joham did not like Kandimba's answer. He realized Kandimba and his warriors had not been sent to support the mercenaries. Their job was to kill them all if they did not succeed.

"We will succeed," Joham said. "I have no doubt of that."

"We shall see, Portuguese," Kandimba replied.

- 5 -

Caungula sat among the elders of Cilombo, discussing the matters of the day. Time had been harsh to Changa's cousin. Though he still possessed the size and strength of their common bloodline, his graying hair and beard reflected the stress of his position as kabaka of the citadel city. He listened as the farmers demanded new lands to cultivate for the fields atop the hill were losing their vitality despite diligent rotation. There were also complaints of living spaces. Cilombo was no longer a refuge. It had bloomed into a city, its population exceeding its capacity. Caungula weighed the words of each speaker and gauged the reactions of the elders before he spoke. The council house finally fell silent as he raised his hand, holding the wooden scepter designating his rank. The audience looked to him in anticipation of his decision. He closed his eyes as he recalled every argument. Lifting his head and opening his eyes, he stood then walked to the center of the house.

"Cilombo was never meant to be a permanent city," he said, his voice filling the space with little effort. "We came here to organized and fight Usenge, but of late we've done very little of that."

Speaking such words wounded the kabaka. The sorcerer's forces had not assaulted the citadel in over ten seasons, apparently no longer seeing them as a threat.

And in many ways, he was right. Caungula knew he could not defeat the Ndoki pawn unless he procured the ancestors' blessing and that had not occurred. Why, no one knew. A darker memory came to mind, that of the first time Usenge attacked Cilombo and almost destroyed it. He was a young man then, assigned to train and protect Mfumu's heir, his cousin Changa. He remembered the day Changa came to them under Livanga's protection. He was a scared little boy yet full of anger. They only had a short time to train him before Usenge sent his tebos. The last he saw of Mfumu's son was the boy escaping with Livanga. Caungula was one of the few to survive the attack. They buried the others, including his father and Livanga. Changa's body was never found. It was that day Caungula dedicated himself to earning the ancestors' blessing and destroying Usenge. In the meantime, he led the effort to rebuild Cilombo. The city fortress had repelled numerous attacks since then, the lone blemish in Usenge's plans.

A spark of hope always flared in his mind whenever he thought of the ancestors' refusal to grant him their strength. Could it be that the ancestors had not chosen a new kabaka because Changa was still alive? Reality doused the hope as it always had. Too many years had passed. There was a very slight chance the boy could have survived the bush alone, and if he had he was most likely adopted by another people or captured and used as a servant. Mfumu's bloodline was dead. Of that he was sure.

Caungula dispensed with the tasks of the day then set out on his inspection of the city. It was a ritual that had lost its purpose, but it was one tradition of many that were still performed in respect of the ancestors and the original purpose for the city. The lookout towers were still maintained though it had been years since they'd been manned. Granaries were kept full in case of the siege that would never come and the armory remained filled with spears, arrows, knives and swords. Many of the weapons had long past their usefulness; Caungula would periodically have the young warriors discard the rusted and decaying weapons then order the blacksmiths and weapons master to produce more.

Although the marital personality of Cilombo had dissipated the city thrived. Family compounds covered the entire summit, the roads always full with people going about their daily business. Fields of sorghum and cassava rimmed the edge of the summit, fed by the frequent mists and rain. Farmland had also been cleared around the base of the hill, something that would not have been allowed during the city's martial days. Thankfully the wells were abundant and clean, and the nearby river served as another source of water and food.

Caungula was returning to his compound when he spotted the commotion ahead. A crowd gathered before the city market; before he reached it one of his bodyguards ran up to him, a dazed look on his face.

"What is it, Mafuta?"

"It is a messenger," Mafuta replied.

Caungula was stunned.

"A messenger?"

"Yes. He has come from Kitoko."

Caungula pushed by Mafuta. The messenger sat on the ground, bleeding from various wounds throughout his body. He had survived the traps set on the hillside, something that would not have been possible when the devices had been well maintained. Caungula crouched before the man.

"Who are you?" he asked. "Why have you come here?"

The man took a deep breath before answering.

"I am Zima, from Kitoko. I bring joyous news."

"Joyous news?" Caungula rubbed his chin. "What? Is Usenge dead?"

Zima smiled. "No, but he soon will be. The son of Mfumu has returned."

Caungula's skepticism turned into shock.

"What did you say?"

The messenger stood, a proud smile forming on his face.

"I said, the son of Mfumu has returned!"

Caungula grasped the man by the shoulders.

"How can you be sure? He was but a boy when he fled into the bush. I knew him."

"The elders have confirmed his identity," the messenger said. "That is why I was sent. He has gathered an army to fight Usenge. They are on their way here."

Caungula turned to Mafuta.

"Prepare the city!" he said. "We must be ready for Changa's arrival."

Caungula hurried back to his house, dancing as he entered. Ikoko, his great wife, watched him in confusion.

"What is going on?" she asked. "What is wrong with you?"

Caungula hugged her then kissed her.

"Changa is alive!" he said. "He is coming to Cilombo!"

Ikoko pushed him away.

"You are mad!" she replied. "Changa is dead. He died long ago. You know this."

"No, he is alive! A messenger has just arrived. He says Changa has returned and he is leading an army to meet us."

"This is a trick," Ikoko said. "Usenge is behind this."

"I don't think so," Caungula said. "I believe it's true. Changa's body was never found. He is the son of a kabaka, so his nyama is strong. He has come back, Ikoko. He has come back!"

A sound like thunder broke their conversation and the ground shook. Caungula and Kitoko rushed outside. The cries reached them as people rushed toward the edge of the hill. As they ran there was a distance thunder-like sound. Moments later a large object fell among the runners, knocking many of them to the ground. It exploded, sending people and dirt flying into the air. Caungula could not move as he watched the terrible objects tear his city apart like dry leaves. It took a moment for his mind to clear and a grim reality to settle inside him.

"Usenge," Caungula said. He turned to his wife.

"Gather the sorcerers," he said. He donned his armor, took his shield and weapons then ran to the edge of the hill. The war drums boomed as he hurried, his warriors running to him. The objects continued to fall and explode, causing panic, death and confusion throughout the city. When he finally reached the edge Caungula was not surprised at what he saw. The villages at the base of the hill were under attack by Tukuju. The half-dead minions of Usenge trudged through the streets, hacking and slashing with rigid discipline. Those who could not fight took to the paths leading to the city, careful not to spring the traps that only the inhabitants of Cilombo were aware. Further beyond the villages stood another rank of men, their pale faces and odd clothing standing out from the vegetation. Caungula had heard rumors of these men and now he saw them face to face. Before them were objects that resembled metal tubes on wheels. He watched as one of the men stuffed a package into the tube, then another rolled a heavy metal sphere into it as well. The third man touched the back of the tube with a torch, causing an explosion and a dense cloud of smoke. Moments later another blast rocked the city. Caungula had never seen a weapon like this before. These were the objects spitting out the metal that was destroying his city. Usenge had conjured these ghost men and their evil weapon and sent them to destroy his city.

"Djito!" Caungula called out. His general appeared by his side, a grim look on his face.

"Gather the sorcerers. Make sure they are ready to deal with the Tukuju. I will take warriors with me down the hill. We will deal with the pale ones."

Djito ran away shouting orders. Caungula ran as well, heading for the opposite side of the city to the secret trail that led to the base of the hill. He flinched with each discharge, the vision of destruction fueling his limbs. His warriors ran to him and followed, each trained from childhood for the task they were about to perform, secretly hoping that it would never have to be done. The warriors reached the edge of the hill then barreled down the trail, deftly dodging the numerous traps that would kill or maim any intruder unaware of their presence. Soon they were at the base of the hill, running as fast as the bush would allow. Their journey would take them longer than they would like, but it would put them at the rear of the warriors with the deadly weapons. Though they kept deep enough in the bush to remain hidden, they ran close enough to the edge to observe the Tukuju attack on the hill. Usenge's minions climbed the heights with no concern for their personal being; the traps they sprang damaged them but did not deter them. Only the incantations hurled upon them by the sorcerers seemed to stop them, but they were not enough. Caungula and his men had to stop the attack from the pale men's weapon soon or all would be lost.

They were almost to their objective when they heard the twang of bowstrings. Caungula and the others quickly fell into the evasive movements that every ba-Kongo warrior knew from instinct then prepared for the attack sure to follow. Caungula had just settled when the first warrior attacked him. He blocked the sword thrust then stomped the man's foot, momentarily distracting him as he slashed his throat. He smiled as the man fell to the ground; at least they were real men, not Tukuju. This was an opponent he could handle. His relief was short-lived as more warriors appeared. There were too many of them for his small force to handle. Caungula unsheathed his dagger then plunged into the battle. There would be no victory this day. All he could do was prepare for the judgment of the ancestors.

He diverted a spear thrust meant for his throat with his dagger as he sliced his attacker across the chest with his sword. Another warrior crashed into him, knocking him off balance. He turned ready to attack but met the gaze of one of his own. The man smiled then a sword emerged from his stomach. He collapsed, replaced by an enemy warrior. Caungula cut the man's head off then jumped over his thrashing body into a tangle of warriors impeded by the thick brush. He fought with desperate fury, slashing, kicking and biting anyone that came close, ignoring the cuts and stabs he received in return. Weakness crept into him as his blood flowed out of him. His legs threatened to give way but Caungula refused to fall. He stumbled to a sturdy tree then backed against it as he continued to fight off his attackers. The fate of Cilombo was beyond his power now; all he could do was defend himself.

"Stop!"

Caungula's attackers ceased their assault. They backed away in unison, forming a ragged semicircle. Caungula prepared himself for another wave of attacks but it did not occur. The masked warriors separated and a man wearing a red mask crowned by white feathers approached him, sword and shield in his hands. He stopped a few steps away from Caungula, studying him through his eye slits. Although he wore a mask of rank, Caungula knew it was not Usenge.

The man attacked. Caungula fought him as best he could, but he knew this man would claim his life. He was too weak to continue to fight at such a pace. He was dodging the man's sword when something struck his head. There was bright light and then nothing.

* * *

Kandimba stood over Caungula, a grin hidden under his mask.

"Pick him up," he ordered. "Usenge will be pleased."

A messenger arrived as the other warriors tied Caungula. He took off his mask, revealing the smile on his face.

"The Tukuju have captured the city," he said. "They await your command."

Kandimba reached under his leather armor and took out a round whistle. He blew it three times then put it away. The Tukuju would hear the signal and cease their carnage.

"Go inform the Portuguese. Let Joham he and his men can claim their captives," Kandimba said. "We have what we came for."

The messenger prostrated before Kandimba then hurried off to carry out his orders. Kandimba watched as his men secured Caungula then place him into a hammock. They lifted the hammock onto their shoulders.

"Let the Portuguese take who they wish. Whoever they don't take, kill them. We are done here."

Kandimba turned then marched away, followed by his warriors bearing his captive. They faded into the bush as Cilombo burned.

-6-

They came from throughout the Kongo, all heeding Lusati's call. Some came in hunting parties of two or three, others in groups numbering in the hundreds. In a few cases entire cities arrived, singing or chanting with their drums. The rumor had been confirmed; Changa Diop was home.

Changa sat outside Lusati's compound watching, his anxiety increasing every day. His life had been a hard teacher, placing him in almost every situation imaginable and imbuing him with experience that many could never endure. But never before had he been a savior. For most of his adult life he'd imagined returning to the Kongo to avenge his father's death and free his mother and sisters, but he never considered the consequences of his actions on others. Many baKongo had waited on his return. Now that he was here they expected him to lead them to freedom from Usenge's oppressive rule. The dream was easy; the reality was daunting.

"Changa?"

Changa looked into Lusati's questioning face. He forced a smile as he greeted the selima.

"Are you ready?" Lusati asked.

"Yes," Changa replied.

"Then you are a better baKongo than I am," Lusati confessed. "A great responsibility has been placed upon your shoulders, one that I would not care to have."

"Believe me, it is a burden I would not have chosen," Changa replied. "But I've led many before and I have served at the side of a few great men. I am ready."

"Then let us meet your army," Lusati said.

They left Lusati's compound surrounded by his best warriors. No sooner had they began their procession did the villagers surround them, singing Changa's praises and playing their drums to herald his arrival. Their destination was the huge camp that sprang up outside the village like grass during the first rains. As they drew closer those in the camp took up the chant and the drumming. The entire valley seemed to sing and dance.

Lusati led them to a nearby ancestor tree. Changa and the selima sat before the tree, the warrior flanking them on either side. The visitors came forward led by their respective selimas. They prostrated before Lusati and Changa, introducing themselves and their clans. Each boasted of their prowess and their hatred of Usenge, and each described in great detail how they would serve Changa. Changa smiled at each of them and gave his thanks. The greetings lasted the entire day and well into the night. Torches were lit to provide light for the night praises and cooking pots set up nearby to feed the hundreds of people who had come to witness the uniting of the baKongo against Usenge. By the time the greetings ended it was too late to discuss the issue, so the baKongo retired for the night.

The next day began with more arrivals. It was obvious to Changa that they would have to leave Lusati's valley before the visitors consumed its harvest. Soon after the morning meal a council of elders was convened.

"We must move," Changa said to the elders and lesser leaders. "There are too many here for the valley to support."

"You are right, Changa," Lusati said. "My people are happy that you all have come, but we cannot feed and house such a population for long."

One of the new arrivals stood, a warrior who led the largest group of fighters to the valley. He was of mid-height yet of stout body. The scarification he displayed was impressive and intimidating, as was that of his followers.

"I am Bizimana. Me and my warriors have traveled far to fight Usenge. But we know we cannot just march into his city without a plan. Our sorcerers have prepared us for battle against him, but we must fight as one when we meet his forces. We must train together."

"We thank you for your support, Bizimana," Changa replied. "And everything you say is true. But what use is training if we are starving? We will train as we march. The marching itself will be an opportunity to work together. When we reach Usenge's city we will be an army the entire Kongo will fear."

A positive murmur spread among the warriors.

"If it is settled we will use the remainder of this day to prepare for our journey. We will leave first thing next sunrise."

"I will leave runners to guide any that arrive after our departure," Lusati added.

"Wait!"

Kaihemba pushed his way through the gathering to stand before Changa, Lusati and the Elders. He was disheveled as always, but his face possessed seriousness not often displayed.

"We are not going anywhere!" he shouted.

Bizimana and the others looked at the old man, visibly annoyed.

"Who is this man?" Bizimana asked.

Kaihemba rushed to Bizimana, bumping his chest against the warrior. Bizimana's cohorts sprang to their feet in response to the insult but Bizimana waved them down.

"I am the voice of the ancestors!" Kaihemba said. "It was I who discovered the Ghost of Mfumu wandering our woods and brought him to us. The ancestors have shared their wisdom with me on all matters pertaining to his destiny. And I speak for them when I say that we cannot go!"

"And why is that?" Changa asked.

Lusati rolled his eyes. "Why do you humor him Changa? Especially now. We are wasting time."

"Kaihemba was the only one of you who believed who I was when I first came," Changa replied. "I will hear what he has to say."

Changa nodded toward Kaihemba and the elder shared his ragged smile.

"Why must we wait, Kaihemba?" he asked.

"We must wait for her," he said.

Lusati suddenly stalked toward Kaihemba.

"You've gone too far," he said. "Say one more word and I'll kill you."

"I don't fear you Lusati," Kaihemba said. "We cannot march without her. We cannot win without her."

Lusati's hand gripped his sword hilt.

"We do not need her and we never have," he said. "Changa is here now. We will march in the morning as decided."

"We will all die without…"

Lusati's fist smashed against Kaihemba's jaw. The old man collapsed at the kabaka's feet. Changa ran to him, glaring at Lusati as he lifted the old man from the ground.

"Why did you do this?" Changa asked.

Lusati hesitated as if to answer but turned and stomped away.

Bizimana and the others seemed satisfied by Lusati's punishment of Kaihemba. They scattered to their camps to begin preparations. Changa carried Kaihemba to the healers who reluctantly began treating the old man. No one would meet Changa's eyes or attempt to explain Lusati's actions. He would have to find out for himself.

He hurried immediately to Lusati's house. The kabaka was seated before his fire.

"I was expecting you," he said.

"Why did you hit Kaihemba?" Changa asked. "And who is 'she'?"

Lusati turned to Changa.

"I hit him because he is a fool who does not know when to keep his mouth shut," Lusati replied. "I know you have some respect for him, but we have suffered Kaihemba all our lives. Yes, sometimes the ancestors do share their wisdom with him, but no more than with anyone else. There are wise ones more reliable."

"You still haven't told me who 'she' is. It seems that is information no one is willing to discuss."

Lusati gestured for Changa to sit. Changa saw the beer pot sitting beside the kabaka. He offered Changa a straw and he accepted. Changa drank the bitter brew as Lusati spoke.

"Usenge thought that when he killed your father the baKongo would accept him as our ruler. He was wrong. We gathered our warriors as we do now to fight him. Everyone, except Vatukemba. When the messenger arrived in her city she sent them away. She said if Usenge defeated Mfumu it was the ancestors will. She would not go against the ancestors."

Changa could see the anger in Lusati's face.

"Her army was large," he continued. "And her warriors are among the best of baKongo. Some say they are unmatched. If she had marched with us we may have stood a chance. Instead we were defeated. Many of our cities were destroyed. Many more became Usenge's slaves, at least those who were lucky. Others were converted to Tukujus."

"What happened to Vatukemba's and her people?" Changa asked.

"Vatukemba sent emissaries to Usenge to accept his sovereignty," Lusati said. "Emissaries!"

Lusati seethed. Changa did not urge him to continue, seeing that the hate he held for Vatukemba was deep. Lusati took a long sip of his beer, which seemed to calm him. A smile as bitter as the beverage came to his face.

"In return for her gestures Usenge sent his Tukuju. But as I said, Vatukemba's warriors were better than most. They turned back the Tukuju assault. Vatukemba did not wait for another. When the Tukuju returned she and her people were nowhere to be found."

"Has anyone heard from them since?" Changa asked.

Lusati shook his head. "It is rumored that she and her people fled beyond the river valley and built new cities. No one has traveled to confirm it. No one wishes to associate with her if she still lives."

"So, it seems you were angry over nothing," Changa said.

Lusati glared at Changa.

"You have been gone for a long time, Son of Mfumu," he said. "There is much you have probably forgotten and much you never learned. One thing you will discover is that we baKongo don't let go of our hate easily. Even if Vatukemba and her people are no more, we hate the memory of her as much as we do the person that once was."

Changa handed Lusati his drinking straw then stood to leave.

"Thank you for your wisdom," he said.

Changa left Lusati's camp in contemplation. Despite what Lusati told him Vatukemba intrigued him. He did not see her actions as betrayal; he saw them as a leader attempting to protect her people. She'd made the wrong decision, but she had put her people before all others. They could use as many warriors as they could find, but it seemed the link between Vatukemba and the others had been broken too long.

Despite Lusati's story Changa was still concerned about Kaihemba. He did not think the man as deranged as others. He'd encountered many that spoke for the ancestors in his safaris and he knew such a duty rendered a person odd to those around them. Changa could understand why. A person with direct contact with the ancestors and gods must be unique to communicate with those of such wisdom and power. When he reached the healing compound he immediately began searching for Kaihemba. A woman approached him as she wiped blood from her hands.

"You're looking for that fool Kaihemba?" she asked.

"Yes," Changa answered.

"He's gone. Good riddance to him," she said.

"Did he say where he was going?" Changa asked.

"He said he was going to find her. He said he would bring her back just like he brought you back."

"I thank you," Changa said.

He walked away from the compound. There was nothing else he could do for Kaihemba. He was in the ancestors' hands. He headed for his compound to prepare for the march to Cilombo.

Son of Mfumu

- 7 -

The Kongo army made slow progress through the dense forest, the path they followed barely visible. They were few in number, but their purpose carried more weight than a gathering of thousands. Changa walked at the center of the group, led by Enyama and followed by warriors and bearers. The journey to Cilombo would take some days and take him further from his objective for returning; killing Usenge and freeing his family. But the others insisted that this trip was necessary, for no matter how powerful Changa was, he was still a man. He would need an army to confront the nefarious sorcerer and this safari to Cilombo would secure him that.

They set up camp on the summit of a forested hill to prevent flooding of the camp in case of rain. Changa helped despited the protests of his cohorts. He was not kabaka and he would not be treated as such. Here in the forests of the Kongo he would act as he did on the deck of his dhows, lending a hand when necessary. That night they shared a meal of sorghum and the flesh of a bush deer felled by one of their hunters. As the others bedded down for the night Changa remained awake, staring into the embers of the dying fire. He hears movement then looked up to see Enyama approaching. The warrior sat down before Changa then offered him a strip of dried meat. Changa accepted and the two chewed together.

"You have been many places," Enyama said. "Yet you come back to the Kongo. Why?"

"As I said before, long ago I vowed to kill Usenge. Now I'm here to fulfill that vow."

"Many people have tried," Enyama said. "Many have failed. That is why we hide from him and his masters."

"The Ndoki?" Changa asked.

Enyama nodded. "Many think that Usenge rules us, but it is they that pull his strings. He is their dog."

"How do you know this?" Changa asked.

"My grandmother was a sorcerer. She taught us the ways of the world. She showed us the power in the plants and animals surrounding us and she taught us of what spirits to pay honor to. She also taught us of the Ndoki, sorcerers who have given up their bodies to live as immortal animals. She said Usenge wished to be one of them, but instead they sent him back into the world to rule us and serve them. She said this is why he hates us so much."

"He hates me because my baba denied him what he felt should have been his," Changa said. "This is what the Khwe told me."

Enyama's eyes widened. "You have seen the Khwe?"

"Yes," Changa replied. "When I first landed. They saved my life and guided me to Kongo. Their leader, Shasa, gave me this."

Changa raised his arm, displaying the simple bracelet around his wrist. Enyama leaned away from him, fear in his eyes.

"A talisman from the Khwe is a powerful item," he said. "It is a miracle enough that they did not kill you and eat you. They enjoy the flesh of strong warriors. That is what my grandmother told me."

Changa laughed. "Yet I sit here before you with all my flesh still on my bones. Your grandmother was a wise woman, but I think some of what she taught you was not all accurate."

Changa saw the warrior's eyes narrow. The last thing he wanted was an enemy among the people who were helping him.

"Maybe those who told her of the Khwe were misinformed," he added.

Enyama tilted his head as he considered Changa's words.

"That is true," he finally said. "My grandmother had never ventured beyond our land as you have."

"Travel does not make a person wise," Changa replied. "That only comes if that person pays attention during the safari."

Enyama nodded, then yawned and stretched.

"We should rest tonight," he said. We still have a long journey before us, and the way will get much steeper."

"Good night then, Enyama," Changa said.

Changa found a dry spot near a large tree then lay down to rest. He quickly fell into a dream of the sea. He stood at the bow of a dhow heading into a vast horizon. He looked to either side and saw Panya, Mikaili, The Tuareg and Zakee standing with him, each of them sharing a smile. He gazed toward the horizon and his joy faded. As the dhow sailed the sky darkened, churning clouds forming overhead. The sea became choppy and his companions disappeared one by one until Changa stood along facing a black sky and a stormy sea. The howling wind twisted the clouds into the shape of a war mask. Bolts of lighting flared from the eye slits.

"You cannot escape me, son of Mfumu!" the mask shouted. "I will drink your blood as I did your father's!"

Changa sprang from the ground, his knives in his hands just in time to meet the white figure swooping toward him from the dark forest. The faint light of his fire revealed its features; its face resembling that of a wild dog. Wide bat-like wings extended from its back. Changa threw the knife in his right hand, striking the beast's shoulder. It screeched through its fangs then twisted as it flapped its wings. Before Changa could dodge the creature it clamped its claws into his shoulders then lifted him off the ground. Changa grimaced as the claws bit into his flesh. He stabbed up into the creature's abdomen and the beast shuddered as it screeched again. It dropped him and he crashed into the shrubs below. Changa lay stunned for a moment then struggled to his feet. Chaos surrounded him as more bat-like creatures swooped into the camp, the warriors defending themselves with spears and swords. The large creature that attacked Changa continued circling, its cries echoing around them. Its cohorts responded, breaking their attack then joining the large bat thing in flight.

"Everyone to me!" Changa shouted. The warriors gathered around him, fear clear in their eyes.

"Form a circle and raise your spears," he ordered.

"We should run into the woods!" Enyama said. "We are open targets here."

"They came from the woods," Changa replied. "They fly as well there as they do in the open."

He pointed to the large bat creature.

"That's the one we must kill," he said. "It commands the others. It came for me."

"Do you think Usenge sent it?"

"I don't know and it doesn't matter," he said. "What matters is that we kill it."

A series of sharp barks echoed over them and the bat things descended in unison. The warriors threw their throwing spears, bringing two of the creatures down.

Changa rolled free of the others, exposing himself to the large one. It responded immediately, swooping at Changa with its talons open. Changa threw both knives, the spinning blades tearing through the membrane of the creature's wings. It cried as it tumbled from the sky but managed to land before him. The creature was as agile on foot as it was in the air. It swung its wings at Changa, scratching his face and arms. Its reach was too long for Changa to use his sword; he would have to get closer. He dodged the creature's swings and jabs, waiting for the right moment. As the creature swung at him again, Changa remained still as if receiving the blow. The thing screeched in triumph; Changa waited until the claws were almost upon him before ducking the swing then leaping into the beast and tackling it to the ground. The creature flailed and twisted while Changa attempted to get a tight grip on it. Its foul breath stung Changa's nose, its spittle striking his face as it snapped at his head. His throwing knifes were useless as such close quarters; Changa relied on the skills he learned long ago in the Mogadishu fighting pits. The creature twisted suddenly, shaking Changa free; despite its tattered wings it began rising into the sky again. Changa grabbed the bat thing by one of its claws. Heat burned in his stomach then surged throughout his body as he pulled the beast back to the ground. Kintu's Gift had been triggered by the struggle and Changa was grateful for its presence. Many years ago, during the quest for the Jade Obelisk, Changa encountered Kintu. The demi-god shared a portion of his power with him and others through an elixir laced with his spittle. Changa could not summon it at will, but it always manifested when he needed it most. He clambered onto the beast's back then scrambled to where its neck should be. His thick arms were barely long enough to wrap around its throat, so he grabbed the creature's long ears with his hands and wrapped his legs around the neck instead. Squeezing his thighs together, Changa gripped the beast with all his strength. The bat thing managed to let out a shriek before Changa cut off its air. The call was answered; Changa's eyes widened as he saw the other creatures break off their attack on the others and fly in his direction.

"Die already!" he shouted, gripping the creature tighter. The beast falters as its minions swarmed around them, nipping at Changa with needle-like teeth and striking him with their claws. With a hard twist he spun bat thing about as it fell, using its dying body as a shield. He let go then rolled away, the beast slamming against the grounds as life fled its form. The warriors reached Changa and the dead beast, driving the other creatures away with their spears. Without their leader the bat things circled further and further away until they dispersing into from where they came.

Changa struggled to stand then stumbled to his weapons. His companions looked at him, their faces expressing their astonishment. Enyama was the first to approach him.

"You killed that thing...with your hands?"

Changa smirked. "I do that sometimes."

Another warrior crept to the beast then poked it with his spear. Assured of its demise, the warrior went to the creature's legs then began severing its claws. The others joined him. Changa sauntered away then sat against a tree, slowly regaining his strength. Enyama came to sit beside him.

"This was Usenge's doing," Changa said.

"What is a tebo?" Enyama asked.

"Spirits sent to kill me," he answered. "Only I can defeat them, either by my hands or with my throwing knives. It is a game he plays with me."

"That game will end soon," Enyama said. "I have never seen such a thing before, a man killing a beast with his hands. There is no way Usenge can stand up to you. If I every doubted who you are that doubt is gone. You are the son of Mfumu."

Changa said nothing. The anxiousness that filled his mind ever since he'd returned home had been replaced by weariness. He was tired of fighting Usenge's minions, tired of running. It was time for this to end, one way or another.

The other warriors approached the two. One of them stepped forward with a small leather pouch.

"The largest of the monster's claws," he said. "It will add to your nyama."

Changa accepted the pouch. "Thank you. I hope that the ancestors deem me worthy of its power."

Changa stood. "We must hasten our journey. Usenge might have other surprises in store. The sooner we reach the elders the better. We'll rest tonight then break camp early. There will be no rest until we reach Kitoko."

Changa and the others attempted to sleep but the events of the day left everyone shaken. They awoke early then set out, their steps swift and determined. Their respites were brief; they relieved themselves and ate on the march. What really drove the entourage to hasten was their unwanted followers. The bat creatures that attacked them followed, flitting about them during the night and trailing them at a distance during the day. For the first few days they kept a diligent watch at night, expecting an attack. But soon they came to realize the beasts were not going to harm them. They seemed interested in only one person in the group: Changa. When Changa noticed their preference he kept away from his companions, walking far ahead or behind them. A strange thought came to him, one that seemed to be confirmed with every passing day. The creatures apparently existed in a social order, where one beast held sway over the others. That beast was the one Changa slew. It would make sense that its death would spark a fight among the beasts for the new dominant animal, but that was not the case. Changa was not one of them, but it seemed that the pack had chosen him, at least for a time.

After another week of travel they entered the Elders forest. The trees and other plants of this region were more organized and structured, a sign that it had been altered by human hands. The trail widened, bordered by flower-bearing bushes and shrubs. Soon their destination loomed before them, towering over the other plants like a giant among insects. The warriors stopped as the Ancestor tree came into full view then prostrated before it, each whispering a personal prayer. Changa mimicked their gesture but did not pray. After the moment of reverence they continued their march. According to the storytellers it was the oldest tree in the forest and arguably the oldest in the world. Its size became more apparent the closer they came; as they entered the clearing ringing the tree its canopy was barely visible. The trunk of the tree stretched wide enough to contain an entire city. Changa spied other groups entering the clearing, as well as shelters ringing the tree. The messengers had done well; the people of the Kongo were gathering to see Mfumu's son.

Changa also notice another change. The bat things had halted at the pasture's border. He stopped for a moment, watching them circle about for a time before flying into the distance. He assumed either their infatuation with him had come to an end or their were forces at work in the vicinity that drove them away. Most likely it was a combination of both, he surmised. He shrugged then trotted to catch up with the others.

It was their group that drew the most attention as they approached the great tree. The others slowed their pace, their eyes transfixed on Changa. The random march became a procession, the others lining up behind Changa's group. Enyama grinned like a child, apparently pleased to be receiving such attention. For Changa it was a situation he was used to, though he could not deny this particular procession meant more to him than any he'd been a part of before. This was the beginning of his vengeance.

The elders sat on their stools, their complacent faces masking any emotion they may have felt. Changa counted eleven, six men and five women. The woman sitting in the center of the group wore a thick tangle of red and white beads about her shoulders, a sign of her years and experience. The others looked to her as Changa approached; her eyes focused on Changa. They were a few feet away from the elders when the woman raised her palm. Their group stopped in unison then prostrated before the old ones.

"He who claims to be the son of Mfumu may stand," the woman said, her voice strong and clear.

Changa came to his feet. The woman looked him over then waved for him to approach. Changa ambled to them then halted before her.

"I am Changa Diop," he said. "Son of Mfumu."

"So you say," the woman replied. "I am Oluina Liahuka. I was an elder when you baba's baba was born, and I have met him more than a few times. You do have his look."

She turned her head slightly. "What say you? Is this Mfumu's son?"

The others murmured their agreement to her words.

"Come closer," she commanded.

Changa stepped closer to Oluina. The elder extended her arms, tracing his body with her palms without touching him.

"Your nyama is strong," Oluima said. "Most is familiar, but I sense strangeness among it as well. Give me your talisman bag."

Changa took the bag from his larger pouch then handed it to Oluima. She loosened the leather strings with delicate fingers then opened the bag. Her eyes widened then narrowed.

"You have been to many lands to collect theses gifts," she said. "Some were given, others were earned. A few are quite recent."

She took the bat thing claws from his bag and her face soured.

"Usenge," she said.

"Yes," Changa replied.

Oluima tossed the claws aside then gave Changa his bag.

"You are indeed Mfumu's son. I was present at your birth. I was asked to read your fate and my words were not well received. I told your baba you would travel far from his side and make a name beyond his realm. I told him he would not live to see what you would become if he did not pay close attention to those he loved. The closest would kill him, I said. Your father banished me from his court because my words did not please him. Yet they came to pass. Mfumu was a great man, but he did not always listen to wise council. If he had heeded my words and others, he would still be alive and Usenge would have never been."

Oluima's words stung but Changa had no reason to refute her claims. He was eight years old when his baba died.

"I wished he had listened," Changa finally said. "If so, we would not be here."

"The Fates wove your thread long ago," Oluima replied. "All that is is as it should be."

She stood then swept her gaze over all that were present.

"Send for the other clans," she said. Her voice was strong and resolute. "We will gather under this tree and accept the Son of Mfumu as our Kabaka. Then we will march on Usenge and rid ourselves of his filth once and for all!"

The warriors cheered as they shook their spears and swords. Changa looked about as different emotions battled inside him. This was not the way he imagined it. He had traveled the world amassing enough wealth to hire an army to claim his rightful place. He lost that wealth, then regained it again. Yet he had come alone with no expectations. Now an army gathered around him, an army of his own people. Panya told him if he returned with an army he would be seen as an invader; to return alone he would be seen as a savior. Once again her foresight had proven true.

Oluima placed a hand on his shoulder.

"It will take time for the clans to gather," she said. "In the meantime we must prepare you for what comes next."

Changa was puzzled. "What do you mean?"

"We have accepted you, but there must be another trial before you can face Usenge."

"I'm ready now," Changa said.

Oluima shook her head. "No you are not. You must go before the ancestors and ask for their help. You cannot defeat Usenge without them."

"If that's what I must do, then I will do it," he said.

"Don't be so confident," Oliuma warned. "You are not the only person capable of leading us against Usenge. Others have walked this path only to be denied the ancestors' blessing. They may reject you as well."

"I am Mfumu's son," Changa said. "I doubt that they will."

Oliuma's eyes narrowed.

"We will see," she replied. "We will see."

- 8 -

The captive lay upon the granite slab, resigned to its fate. Usenge loomed over it, naked except for a simple loincloth. A jagged knife gleamed in his right hand. The creature did not struggle for it had been given an elixir which rendered it immobile and barely conscious. The others in the room were obscured by incense smoke. They had come from the deep forest, abandoning their refuge to witness what was about to occur. Usenge smiled through his mask. The Ndoki were allowing him to take one step closer to joining them.

The young gorilla made a weak effort to break free from the iron grip of the Tukujus holding it still. Usenge plunged the knife into its heart, holding it firm until the beast ceased its struggles and succumbed to death, at least for the moment.

The Ndoki moved in quickly as the Tukujus stepped away. They wrapped the body with herb soaks clothes like spiders preparing to feast. One of the Ndoki lifted the wrapped carcass from the table, cradling it like a child. The tallest of the wood wizards stopped to gaze on Usenge.

"What you have taken will be yours to wear," it said. "Kill Changa and your tasks will be complete."

"I will," Usenge said.

Son of Mfumu

The Ndoki stared at Usenge a moment longer then followed its cohorts.

Usenge wiped the blood from his dagger then tucked it into its sheath. As he exited the ceremonial hut his servants entered with buckets of water to clean the dais. Usenge strode across the clearing to his city, his Tukuju marching single file behind him. The ceremony relaxed him. The Ndoki were finally bringing him closer, a sign of their growing confidence in him. For decades he feared Changa's return, doing everything in his power to kill him before he returned. The Ndoki had watched him, knowing that in order to fully claim his place the son must be killed like the father.

While the Ndoki side of him revelled in his power and control, the vestiges of his humaness were disappointed. For years he'd watched Mfumu praised and loved by his people; he'd seen the love and admiration he's received from his wife and children, especially Changa. Usenge wanted that in his own life, to be loved and needed like the kabaka. His father had died in one of Mfumu's father's many wars; his mother fell into depression so deep he watched her wither away and die a few years later. With both parents dead and no older siblings or relatives to take him in he became an orphan and was eventually adopted by Katahali, Mfumu's uncle. Mfumu and Usenge grew up as cousins, and although Katahali and his family raised him as their own, Usenge still sensed a distance that would never be bridged. Mfumu had been his constant companion as boys, sharing so much together. Still, he could not help but envy him. Mfumu's path was certain, Usenge's was not. As they grew older, envy turned to jealousy, jealousy to hatred.

The time came when the two of them, as well as all the children of their clan, were brought before the elders to learn of their fate. Mfumu's place among them

67

was certain before the elders spoke. He would be the future Kabaka, taking his father's place once the ancestors called him home. Usenge, however, was not pleased by his destiny. Since he was second oldest, his place should have been at Mfumu's side as his advisor and administrator. Such a position would make him the second most powerful person in the realm. While Mfumu concerned himself with the traditional duties and ceremonies of their people, it would be Usenge who truly ran the kingdom. But that was not to be. Mfumu chose Nyindu, the son of his father's friend as advisor. Usenge was to be Nyindu's assistant. It was the final insult. Though Usenge still played the loyal cousin, he simmered in his hatred.

They reached his compound in the center of the city. High stone walls rose from the earth, the only entrance two wooden doors strengthened with iron crosbolts. The men guarding the gate were not Tujuku, nor were they local. They were Zulu mercenaries, men who had lost their *umuzis* and cattle and wandered north to the Kongo hiring out their martial skills. Usenge learned long ago not to trust those among him; those close to him came from far away and served him because of the power and privilege he provided. It was in their best interest to protect him, for their fortunes depended on his life.

His personal servants came to him immediately as he entered the compound. Usenge handed them his items as he strode across the courtyard to his home. His servants went about their chores; tending his fields and animals as they prepared for the evening meal. Though his compound mirrored those of other baKongo, there was one thing noticeably missing; children.

The servants opened the door to his house. Usenge entered to see his greatest reward sitting opposite the door. The former wife and daughters of Mfumu stood then prostrated before him.

"Welcome home, husband," they said in unison. After so many years their voices still contained defiance and disdain. In the beginning it annoyed him; he beat them daily to break their spirits but eventually realized they would die before submitting to him. So he relented.

Usenge stood before the central fire.

"Bathe me," he commanded.

The women scowled as they exited the house, returning moments later with buckets of water, black soap and wash cloths. Mukumba, Mfumu's widow removed Usenge's talisman then set them on the chest beside his bed. She then removed his loincloth. Usenge stood naked, his arms outstretched as the women washed the white chalk from his body. Their hands were rough against his skin, occasionally striking him. Usenge grinned at their feeble efforts to harm him.

They wiped him dry with the cloths. The daughters then prepared his meal while Mukumba rubbed shea butter into his umber skin. She dressed him then placed his talisman around his neck.

"How was your day?" he said, sarcasm heavy in his voice.

"The same as every day," Mukumbu replied.

Usenge gazed at Mfumu's widow and grinned through his mask.

"Paradise," he said.

"It soon will be now that my son has returned."

Usenge's response was reflexive, his hand striking Mukumba across the mouth. The woman staggered back but did not fall. Her daughters flocked around her as she held her mouth, a smile on her face.

"So it is true," she said. "My son has come to avenge his father."

"You shall watch Changa die just as you watched Mfumu," Usenge replied. "All that happened has happened for a reason. Do you think he survived on his own accord?"

Usenge laughed. "He was given time to become a man to gain the ancestors' favor so that when I killed him I would gain his nyama. Once he is dead you and your daughters will be offered as wives to our neighboring allies to cement the bonds. Although you will probably remain. You are too old to be of any use to a young monarch."

"Your threats lost their teeth long ago," Mukumba replied. "The only reason you sit where you are today is because you betrayed the man that loved you like a brother."

"He did not love me!" Usenge shouted. "None of you did!"

Usenge let the rage pass before speaking again.

"It does not matter. I rule the baKongo and when your son is dead I will earn the ancestors' favor. They will have no choice. There will be no other. Leave me."

"With pleasure," Mukumba replied.

Usenge watched Mukumba and her daughters leave the hut, each taking the time to share a venomous stare. He dropped his head once he was sure they were gone. He should have killed them after he killed Mfumu. He had no intentions of making them wives in a true sense for he wanted no children by them. Their presense was to solidify his rule over the baKongo, nothing more. There would be no children from him; he cared nothing of lineage and destiny, at least not now. His goal was to kill Changa and end Mfumu's legacy. Once that was done he would take his place among the Ndoki as an honored one and his true reign would begin.

- 9 -

The entire city turned out for the day's event. For months the men and women standing in the center of the human circle suffered the greatest physical and mental hardships of their lives, all in the name of becoming one of the elite. While the circle chanted and ululated, the families of those final few were the loudest and most animated. The ceremony they were about to witness was a formality, albeit a dangerous one. Even if they did not survive, each one was assured a special place among the ancestors. For a people who valued warriors more than anything else, those standing before them had reached the pinnacle of achievement. When they stepped from the circle, they would be *Siluwe*, 'The Leopards.'

The nine men and women crouched, their eyes shifting as they attempted to determine from where their opponent would enter the circle. Each held a throwing club in their hands with more stuffed in their sashes. While the Siluwe were adept with all forms of hand combat and weapons, it was the throwing club in which they excelled. A Siluwe could fell a bird from the sky with a club; a shower of war clubs from a Siluwe war party was like a storm of stones, pounding their hapless opponents into submission. Each of them had witnessed this ceremony from the ring; they knew their opponent lurked behind the celebrants, waiting for the right time to strike.

A piercing cry silenced the circle. A person som-
ersaulted over the ring, landing upright on both feet then
immediately sprinting for the neophyte Siluwe. Two
clubs streaked toward the warriors before they were
aware and two of them were struck in the head, crum-
bling unconscious to the ground. The others turned to
their attacker, throwing their clubs. The opponent twisted
its body with incredible dexterity and flexibility, dodging
the projectiles. It threw its clubs as well and the warriors
contorted to avoid them with much less grace. The spec-
tators roared in approval; the ceremony had begun. The
opponent flitted among the warriors like a deadly moth,
throwing clubs and using them as a bludgeon when close
enough. The warriors went down one by one, some unconscious, others disabled by bruises and broken bones.
None lamented their wounds. The healers would repair
them and each was proud to be where they were despite
the beating they took. Their families rushed in to remove
them from the battlefield, raising them high and cheering
their success.

Soon only the opponent and one warrior remained. Kifunji's family danced among the ring, their
pride immeasurable. Kifunji fought to contain her joy.
To be the last to stand before the personification of their
name was to be the most honored of her group. It was
also the most dangerous of the ceremony. To face
'Mama Siluwe' alone was to face death itself. She would
decide if you lived or died.

"My life is yours," Kifunji said as she swayed
from side to side before Mama Siluwe.

Mama attacked. Kifunji barely avoided the club,
the hardened wood festooned with Siluwe teeth grazing
her head and drawing blood. The flat of Mama's foot
sank into her stomach, knocking her breathless. She
dropped to her knees, gasping for breath. She fell to her
left, barely avoiding the club strike meant for the crown

of her head. Darkness settled into her mind as her breath came to her. Mama Siluwe had decided. She was to die.

But Kifunji had also decided that if she was to die, it would be a grand death that all would remember. She twisted her body then flung out her leg, tripping Mama Siluwe. The crowd gasped as Mama hit the ground. Kifunji clambered to her feet the fell upon her opponent, striking with clubs in both hands. Mama Siluwe blocked most of the blows, managing to regain her feet. They battled toe to toe, their club duel a brutal dance as they spun, cart wheeled and twisted to gain advantage against each other. The blows were taking their toll on Kifunji but she continued to battle. The sound of the celebrants was the loudest she'd ever heard, which fueled her to fight on.

A club smashed against her face. Kifunji heard a crunching sound and pain shot through her jaw as her mouth fell open. She fell to her knees, the pain blinding. Still, she attempted to stand. A hand grasped her shoulder, pushing her back to her knees.

"Enough," Mama Siluwe said. "This fight is over."

Mama Siluwe went to her knees as well to face Kifunji. She took off her leopard mask, revealing her stern yet handsome face. The circle fell completely silent; even the drummers' hands went still.

"You have done well, daughter," she said. "Never before has a new Siluwe fought so skillfully and so bravely. I see the future in your eyes. One day you will be Mama Siluwe."

If Kifunji could talk she would have said so many things. Instead she merely nodded as she tried to hold her mouth in place.

Mama Siluwe stood, pulling Kifunji to her feet. She raised Kifunji's free hand and the crowd cheered. Kifunji's family ran into the circle as Mama Siluwe stepped away to allow them their moment. They lifted her onto their shoulders, parading her around the circle as those of her class that could joined them, their families close behind. Soon the ring disintegrated into a mass dance fueled by the drummers and singers. Kifunji peered over the throng, watching Mama Siluwe walk away, rubbing her torso as if in pain. She grinned; she had done well. She finally relaxed, succumbing to the searing pain of her broken jaw then passing out in the joyous hands of her family.

Vatukemba's servants were waiting when she returned to her palace. Her noble stride had degenerated to a painful stagger as she entered her compound, her condition hidden from others by the wall of guards surrounding her. Each Siluwe ceremony was more difficult than the last but Vatukemba refused to allow anyone else the honor of initiating the final candidates. It was her duty as Mama Siluwe to transition her cubs to warriors and she would share it with no one else.

Bifuasa ran from the palace followed by her apprentices. She wrapped her thick arms around Vatukemba's waist then lifted the woman off her feet, carrying her like a newborn. She was the only person Vatukemba would let handle her in such away. She had saved her life many times, although this situation was not nearly as serious.

"When will you stop this foolishness?" Bifuasa scolded.

"When I sit among the ancestors," Vatukemba replied.

"That may be next initiation."

"They are becoming more skilled," Vatukemba commented.

"And you are getting older," Bifuasa retorted. "Time is the ultimate Siluwe. It always wins."

"But not yet," Vatukemba said. "Besides, you will fix me as you always do."

"There are some things I can't fix, like stubbornness."

Vatukemba rolled her eyes. "I'm tired of your fussiness. I'm your kabaka, not your child. Do your duty and leave me be."

"Should I drop you then, my kabaka?"

"Drop me in your vat of healing herbs then leave me be."

"That I will gladly do. I'll leave one of my apprentices with you as well just in case your head sinks below the water and a new kabaka is required."

Vatukemba laughed then quickly regretted it as pain flashed from her ribs. They entered the palace, hurrying through the various chambers before reaching the high wooden doors of her private quarters. The guards flanking the doors opened them for the group, revealing a spacious yet sparse chamber. The stone healing tub was visible at the far end, servants pouring the final amounts of Bifuasa's healing elixir into the granite vat. Bifuasa set Vatukemba down on the rim of the tub and the kabaka undressed. Bifuasa grimaced as she watched.

"This is worse than most," she said. She reached out then touched a bruise on Vatukemba's left side. Vatukemba flinched.

"Your rib is broken," Bifuasa said. "My herbs will do nothing for that."

"You can tend to it later," Vatukemba replied. "For now, let me rest. Tell Keise the compound is in his hands until I relieve him."

"Yes, kabaka."

Vatukemba moaned as she eased into the bath. She floated to her head rest the lay her head on the leather wrapped cushion. The tingling she felt on her skin assured her the herbs were working and she closed her eyes, falling into a deep sleep.

*   *   *

When Vatukemba awoke it was morning. Flickering torchlight illuminated the room, the smell of fragrant wood and oil teasing her nostrils. She pulled herself from Bifuasa's concoction then stepped into an open robe held by an apprentice. Her pains were either gone or diminished, all except the broken rib. Her walk was slow yet steady as she crossed the expanse of her private chamber. For twenty years Vatukemba had ruled her realm. She began with just a handful of people in a strange land and built it to a vast dominion of hundreds of treks and thousands of people. Some came because of the safety and stability her rule offered; some because they had been defeated by her army and absorbed into the realm. Even to those subjugated she was fair; their tribute was not excessive and her laws protected all equally. Despite her success, there was still one possession that eluded her, one that remained far from her grasp because of a powerful sorcerer and fastidious ancestors.

Vatukemba's children were waiting for her when she entered the family chamber. They gathered about her like the babies they no longer were. Each had their own families and compounds and each had earned high stations among her council. All were more than capable of their duties; they knew Mama Siluwe would have it no other way. They followed her to her stool then sat on the floor cushions around her as they did when they were much younger. Mpata, her eldest, spoke first.

"Mama, when will you stop this stupid ceremony?" she asked.

"You've been talking to Bifuasa," Vatukemba replied. "You shouldn't."

"I don't need Bifuasa to tell me that you are getting too old to play with the Siluwe. We were all at the ring. We saw you and Kifunji duel."

Vatukemba smiled. "Yes. She is good. Almost as good as you."

Mpata smiled. Vatukemba always threw Mpata off her rants with compliments. The woman liked praise too much.

"Thank you, mama, but your platitudes will not work this time. It is time you either stopped the ceremony or have someone else perform the initiation."

"The ceremonies will not cease," Vatukemba replied. "They are vital to the training of the Siluwe and the core of our warriors' pride. But say I was to step aside. Who would take my place?"

"I would," Mpata said.

Vatukemba smirked. "I thought so."

Mpata eyes went wide. "It is not what you think, mama."

"She says what we all feel."

Beya, Vatukemba's son, looked at her with the eyes of his father, her favorite husband. He was the charmer of the family, the one with kind words and easy manners that made all love him, which explained his large number of wives and children.

"I'm not in the mood for your sweet words, Beya," Vatukemba said. "Be quiet." The best way to avoid his charms was not allowing him to speak. No one knows a childlike its mother.

"Then let me speak," Tshishimba said.

Everyone looked at Vatukemba's youngest in surprise. The timid girl rarely spoke during the family meetings, preferring to share her views in private. She possessed a brilliant mind, serving Vatukemba as her administrator. No one kept order like Tshishimba.

"I think mama should continue doing what she does until she deems it necessary to step aside."

Mpata glared at Tshishimba.

"You finally decide to speak and you say the wrong words."

"I say exactly what I wanted to say," Tshishimba replied. "Whether it is right or wrong depends on perspective. Mama is our kabaka. This realm would not exist without her strength, bravery and judgment. We in this room would not be without her. We owe her everything. If she wishes to continue to fight in the initiation then so be it. As long as she does I will be there to cheer her. If the day comes that she dies in the ring, I will sing her praises and mourn my loss as I carry her body from the ring."

Tshishimba's words, while supportive, were also poignant. Vatukemba had never imagined dying in the ring, yet it was a possibility. She looked into her youngest eyes and Tshishimba stared back at her with the concern Mpata and Beya expressed.

"I will consider it," Vatukemba said. "Although I feel I have many seasons left in me to fight in the ring, it is true that time has dulled my skills. But I will be the one who decides when that time has come."

Her children nodded in compliance.

"Now, let us discuss other things."

Beya was about to speak when the door opened and Keise strode in, a worried look on his face. Vatukemba knew if her compound keeper intruded on a family meeting it was a serious matter. He prostrated before the royal family then spoke, his head still lowered.

"Kabaka, I beg your pardon and that of the Ancestors for my intrusion."

"What is it, Keise?" Mpata asked.

"There is a disturbance at the city gates," he said.

Vatukemba was puzzled. She could think of nothing her warriors could not handle, not even an unexpected attack.

"Has the wall warriors taken sick?" she said. "Have them handle it."

"I cannot," Keise replied. "This requires your attention."

Vatukemba rose from her stool then strode out of the room.

"Mama!" Mpata called out. "Your clothes!"

Vatukemba returned for her garments then continued to the gate. Keise ran to take his place before her then called out for the palace guard. The Siluwe warriors fell in step with their mother, eyes forward and weapons drawn. They marched through the city, Vatukemba still puzzled about what lay beyond the gate. As she neared she heard yelling like she'd never encountered. It sounded as if a man was being eaten by lion and enjoying it. By the time she reached the ramparts the entire city followed, their murmur competing with the mysterious screaming. As she reached the rampart the screaming ceased. She stared down upon an unkempt elder wearing a cone shaped hat and leaning on a thick staff crowned with a golden elephant figure. The Elder shielded his eyes as he looked up to the ramparts, his yellow orbs meeting Vatukemba's. He let out a yelp of joy.

"Bring me a bow," Vatukemba ordered.

"I see my praise song has captured your attention," the old man said.

"That was a song," she replied. "We thought something was dying."

"What you say is partially true," the old man answered. "For as I stand before you in health, Kongo dies."

The warrior came with the bow and a quiver of poison arrows. Vatukemba waved him off for the moment.

"The fate of the Kongo no longer interests me," she said. "I have my own realm."

"If what you said is true I would not stand here before you," the old man countered. "I see what the ancestors see, and the desire to rule Kongo still burns in you."

Vatukemba did well not to show her shock. As much as she wished to sit upon the Kongo stool she knew it was not a reality; at least not for her.

"The one who is true to the stool has returned," the elder said. "It is time for you to return as well."

Vatukemba's mouth went dry.

"Are you saying that Changa is back?"

"The son of Mfumu has indeed returned. As we speak he has gathered an army to march on Usenge. They march to Cilombo, then to Usenge. You must be with them!"

Vatukemba left the ramparts, followed by her family and her guards.

"Open the gates!" she commanded. By the time she reached the gates they were open, her warriors forming a gauntlet leading to the strange elder. Vatukemba stopped a spear length from the man, waiting for her warriors to form a circle around him. The elder showed no fear, smirking as the warriors took their place. Once they were in position he prostrated before her then quickly regained his feet.

"Who are you?" Vatukemba asked.

"I am Kaihemba, voice of the ancestors. I have come to tell you that the ancestors wish you to join your true people as they march on Usenge."

"How did you find us?" she asked.

"The ancestors, of course," Kaihemba replied. "You did not think you could walk away from your destiny, did you?"

Keise arrived with her stool and she sat. Kaihemba sat as well, plopping down on the dirt and crossing his legs. It was an insult for a common person to sit before the Kabaka without permission, but Vatukemba was too distracted to notice a failure of protocol.

"Tell me, mouth of the ancestors, has Changa received the ancestors' blessing?"

"His return is the blessing that Changa was destined to defeat Usenge!"

Vatukemba smiled. "No. It is not. Changa must undergo the cleansing ritual at the Ancestor tree before he can defeat Usenge. If he has not done so he marches to his death."

"Then it is vital that you come!" Kaihemba said.

"I will do no such thing," Vatukemba replied. "Why should I help those who have not helped me? Let Changa and the others try to defeat Usenge. When they have failed then I will return and do the deed myself."

Kaihemba was dumbfounded for a moment, but realization caused his eyes go wide then narrow.

"If Changa is dead, the ancestors will favor you," he said.

Vatukemba smiled.

Kaihemba leaped to his feet then ran toward the forest. Mpata came to her side.

"Should I kill him?"

Vatukemba shook her head.

"He will not reach them in time," she said. We'll wait for a few weeks then send a scouting party. By that time all should be settled."

"And then?" Mpata asked.

Vatukemba stood then rested her hands on her daughter's shoulders.

"Then we will go to Kongo and claim what is ours."

-10-

The baKongo army emerged from the bush surrounding Cilombo to a terrible sight. The cleared land
between the forest and the hill fortress was littered with
bodies and carrion-eaters. It was a shock to see despite
the signs witnessed along the way, scattered bodies of
baKongo fighters mingled with Usenge's masked warriors. Still, many found it hard to digest. Some prayed,
others cried. Changa did neither. He was used to the
sights of war, having fought in many throughout his safari. He followed Ligongo and the others toward the hill,
the memory of his brief time in the hillside citadel creep-
ing into his mind. He thought of Livanga, his mother's
handmaiden and a warrior in disguise, who spirited him
away to the temporary safety of Cilombo. He remembered his uncle Ngonga, the stoic warrior and founder of
Cilombo. He died with so many others in Usenge's assault on the hill. And then there was his age group led by
his cousin Caungula. He'd assumed all had died in the
attack, but he had been wrong. Caungula now led the
people of Cilombo, or at least used to lead them. Changa
doubted they would find anyone alive.

The villages at the base of the hill had been ravaged. Homes were burned, the remains of the inhabitants
and attackers littering the spaces between compounds.
They came across strange pits in the ground surrounded

by dead bodies. Ligongo knelt beside one, his face twisted in confusion.

"What is this?" he said.

"Cannon blast," Changa replied.

Ligongo turned to him. "What is a cannon?"

"A tube of metal that fires a ball of iron containing explosive power," Changa replied. "The cannon fires the cannon ball which flies through the air then lands on the ground. Soon after it explodes. The iron pieces kill anyone and anything nearby. That's how they took the city."

While many of the warriors searched the base villages for survivors Changa and the others proceeded to the trails leading to the crest of the hill.

"Wait," Ligongo said. "Cilombo trail are known for their traps."

Changa walked by him. "We'll tread where the traps have been sprung."

"How will we do that?"

Changa turned to look at Ligongo.

"We'll walk on the dead."

The warriors began their morbid climb up the mountain, Changa leading the way. The words of the warriors asking forgiveness for defiling the dead reached Changa's ears and he did the same. When they finally reached the summit, the scene was similar to what they witnessed at the base, with one exception. There were survivors. Changa's warriors broke rank, rushing to them. They were met with cries of joy. The warriors immediately shared their provisions and comforted those still bearing wounds from the attack. A group of men limped toward Changa, Ligongo and the other leaders, their faces grim. One man approached them and managed to smile.

"We are glad to see you," he said. "Although as you can see you are a bit late."

"We are so sorry," Ligongo said. "We had no idea Usenge planned to strike."

"No one did," the man replied. "I am Djito, kabaka of Cilombo."

"I am Ligongo."

Ligongo and Djito shook hands. Djito's eyes strayed to Changa.

"Who are you?" he asked.

"I am Changa Diop."

Djito immediately dropped to the ground, prostrating before him.

"Forgive me, Son of Mfumu," he said. "I did not know!"

Changa reached down then lifted the man to his feet.

"There was no reason for you to know, and no reason for you to bow to me. Where is Caungula? Isn't he kabaka?"

Djito's embarrassed expression returned. "Caungula left me in charge of defending the summit while he led warriors against the fire spitters. He did not return."

"So, he is dead?" Changa asked.

"We do not know. His body has not been found."

"Thank you, Djito. How many of your warriors survived?"

"Not many," Djito replied. "The Tukuju attacked. For every one we killed many died. I have ten men healthy enough to fight, another thirty that are injured but will march with you if you command."

"No, you and your men will stay here," Changa said.

"We need all men he can spare," Ligongo said.

"Thirty men won't make a difference with Usenge," Changa replied. "They can stay and help recover."

Changa turned his attention back to Djito. "We will share what provisions we can and help you build up supplies before we move on."

"Thank you, Changa," Djito said. "You are truly your father's son."

Changa and the others continued to inspect the city. It would take much work to rebuild it and Changa and his warriors did not have the time to do so. The same words were echoed by Ligongo.

"Why are we wasting time here," he asked. "We must go!"

"We will stay and do what we can first," Changa said. "I won't leave such a situation behind us. We can at least get them on their feet before moving on. We may need their help on our return."

Ligongo contemplated Changa's words.

"What you say bears wisdom," he finally said. "But we still must limit our time."

"True," Changa agreed. I don't want Usenge's forces to reach him. Pick your best warriors. The rest will stay here. We have a raiding party to catch."

Ligongo's smile revealed his preference.

"At once!" he replied.

The baKongo buried their dead and prayed to the Spirits for their souls. They prayed as well to those enemies killed in hopes that their souls would not linger to torment the living. That night Changa gathered with the warriors and survivors for a solemn meal, his mind once again filled by the memory of his brief stay. The morning brought their purpose back to the forefront as he prepared to lead the pursuit forces after the attackers. Ligongo stayed behind to continue help the people of Cilombo; Changa gathered a group of warriors to him.

"Take only what you can carry," he said. "We'll be moving fast and hard. If you do not feel you are up to it, say so now. No one will be thought lesser because of it."

All the warriors remained. Changa nodded then turned to leave.

"What of the Tukuju?" one of the warriors said.

"I'll handle them," Changa replied.

They set off at a warriors' pace, led by those who had proved their tracking skills earlier. The conditions of the camp indicated the attack occurred only a few days before their arrival; with captives the invaders would travel slow. They also did not know they were being pursued, so there would be no urgency.

The force ran for the entire day. They camped that night then rose at first light the next day, foraging the forest for additional provisions before setting out again. It was midday when the scouts came to Changa with grim looks on their faces.

"Tell me," Changa said.

"They are close," one of the scouts replied.

"How many?"

"Two hundred. They have captives."

"And the Tukuju?"

"Twenty," the scout said, a worried look on his face.

Changa turned to his warriors.

"Usenge's men are close," he said. "We will slow the pace. By tonight we'll be in position to attack."

The men nodded in unison then exchanged concerned looks. Changa studied their faces before speaking. They were eager, but they were also naïve. He was sure of their bravery, but he knew none of them had encountered the type of fight they were about to experience.

"We will either win or die tomorrow," he said. "How this will end is up to us. You do not know me. All you know is a legend. So, I will not ask you to fight for me. Fight to make your ancestors proud. That is all I ask of you."

The pace was slow yet persistent as they closed in on the group. Grim signs of their passage appeared. Bodies of captives unable to keep the pace and warriors too wounded to continue littered the road and the bush. Some captives displayed wounds on the backs, telling the story of their attempts to flee. There would be time to honor their deaths later but for the moment they had to continue. By night fall they were within striking distance. Changa halted the march and the men rested. Changa found the scouts sitting under a large tree cleaning their weapons and eating. They stood immediately as they saw him approaching.

"Finish your meals," he said. "When you are done we will go to the Usenge camp."

The scouts quickly completed their preparation then the trio departed. They followed the road for a time then entered the bush. Their process slowed as they moved forward warily, on the lookout for any scouts or camp guards. The Usenge warriors' confidence continued to weaken their discipline. They encountered no one. The light from numerous cooking fires served as a beacon to the camp. Changa and the scouts worked their way around the perimeter, noting the position of the warriors, the captives, and most of all, the Tukuju. The half-dead warriors sat separate from the others, staring blankly into the sky. Changa's hand went to his throwing knife, Kintu's Gift stirring in his gut. But now was not the time. He signaled the scouts and they eased back to the road, returning to the others before darkness was full upon them. They gathered the others then surrounded the camp, positioning themselves for the attack. As his men rested for the battle to come, Changa did not sleep. He sat up the entire night, watching the Tukuju. He had no idea how the battle would end. Although the baKongo displayed bravery, he longed for his baharia and his old friends. However, that was not to be. Zakee was among the ancestors, Mikaili carried a holy book instead of a sword, and the Tuareg was master of his own realm once again. He smiled as he thought of Panya. Despite her skills she was only person he would not want her, although he knew she would insist to be present. She was too precious to him. There was so much he did not share before he departed, but it would have to wait.

No sooner did the daylight seep through the dense trees did Changa and his men move forward. Changa took out his throwing knives then ran full speed toward the Tukuju. As he advanced the half-men shifted, their heads lowered. As he reached the clearing the Tukuju were rising to their feet, each of them looking in his direction. Changa yelled as he entered the clearing. The throwing knifes flew from his hands, each striking a Tukuju in the forehead. The victims collapsed, thrashing as the souls trapped inside them made their escaped. A hazy mist seeped from their mouths and nostrils. Changa took two more throwing knives from his back sheaths but these he did not throw. Kintu's Gift surged throughout his body as he clashed against the Tukuju ranks, sacred baKongo iron meeting enchanted steel.

The ringing metal was a signal for his cohorts. They plunged into the camp, attacking Usenge's warriors with the fury of a wet season storm. The captives rose to help them, grabbing whatever they could use as weapons to take revenge on their captors. Changa could not help them, for despite being almost dead, the Tukuju moved with the speed and dexterity of normal men. But they were no match for Changa's determined ferocity. He was a blur, dodging and sidestepping the countless blades while severing limbs and heads. He ignored the cuts inflicted on him, knowing that for every Tukuju he killed another hapless person was freed from Usenge's torture.

This was not a fight where surrender was possible. He would have to kill every last one of them.

The final Tukuju fighting him seemed more animated that the others. It matched Changa's speed, but failed to meet his intensity. Moment later it lay before him dismembered, its captive soul dissipating into the morning mist. Changa did not stand to observe his grim handiwork. He ran toward the main camp to assist his warriors. The men they fought were not baKongo, they were pale skinned men from far beyond the region. One man stood out among them, a man dressed in clothing Changa was familiar with. He wielded his sword with skill, handling the warriors as his brethren attempted to organize a retreat. Changa put away his throwing knives and pulled his kashkara sword from its leather sheath. As one of his warriors fell to the man's skillful work Changa took his place. The man attacked Changa immediately and Changa parried his sword. The two dueled as the battle swirled around them, their eyes locked. The man's smile had faded long ago, replaced by a hard look of determination. Changa was about to lunge for a clear opening when he saw the man raise his flintlock pistol with his left hand. Changa sidestepped as the gun fired, the lead ball grazing his cheek. He plunged through the gun's hazy spoor ready to resume the fight, but the man was gone as was his cohorts. Some of his warriors were taking up pursuit when Changa called them back.

Changa sheathed his sword then touched his wounded cheek. The graze was not serious; he would have it tended to later. He wandered among the aftermath, counting his men. They'd done well, especially considering that they had attacked a force much larger than their own. The captives were free, tending themselves and the warriors that rescued them. Changa met Mbuyu, one of Ligongo's ranking warriors, at the center of camp.

"How many did we lose?" Changa asked.

"Ten," Mbuyu replied.

"I hate to lose any warrior, but considering the circumstances we did well. We'll wait for the others before continuing."

"Shouldn't we send warriors after them?" Mbuyu asked. "If they reach the main war party they will warn Usenge that we are coming."

"Usenge already knows," Changa replied. "The moment I fought the Tukuju he knew. He is as much a part of those monsters as the souls of the hapless ones trapped inside them. Send a messenger back to Cilombo. If the others have not begun their march they should. We will do what we can for the captives until they arrive."

"I will do as you say, Changa," Mbuyu said.

Changa turned to help tend to the wounded. His healing skills were not the best, but they were good enough to lend a hand.

"Changa," Mbuyu called out.

Changa looked over his shoulder at the warrior.

"What is it, Mbuyu?"

"I saw you fight the Tukuju," he said. "We all did. The ancestors truly favor you."

"I haven't killed Usenge yet," Changa replied. "You should reserve your opinion of me until then."

-11-

Usenge was waiting when the advance party from the attack on Cilombo arrived. A smile came to his mask as he saw Kandimba and his warriors striding toward him, dragging a man between them. Kandimba prostrated before Usenge then stood, removing his mask to reveal a broad smile.

"Cilombo burns," he said. "The Portuguese weapon was magnificent."

He signaled with his hand and his warriors dragged the captive forward, shoving the man to Usenge's feet. Kandimba grinned like a satiated hyena.

Usenge reached down and wrapped his right hand around Caungula's neck. He lifted the man off the ground, studying his pained face as he strangled him.

"Caungula," he said. "It has been a long time. You seem to be a man, but you are still a boy."

He dropped Caungula then wiped his hands.

"I defeated your father and now you. Your family should have known by now that opposing me is fruitless."

Caungula sat up, rubbing his throat.

"Your day has come," Caungula said. "Changa Diop has returned."

"I have heard," Usenge replied. "It's fitting that the son has come to die as his father did. I would say the same fate awaits you, but that would be a lie."

Caungula froze, his face awash with fear. He jumped to his feet attempting to flee but Usenge's warriors caught him.

"No, you won't die this day," Usenge said. "As a matter of fact, you may never die. The Tukuju seem to be very durable."

"No!" Caungula shouted. "No!"

He fought the warriors but they held him firm.

"Your cousin Changa Diop will come to me and it is only fitting that his relatives are here to greet him."

"He'll kill you!" Caungula shouted.

"No," Usenge replied. "That will not happen. You will make sure that he doesn't."

Usenge looked to Kandimba.

"Take him to the hut. I will be there shortly."

Kandimba and his warriors dragged Caungula away. As they Usenge returned to his stool the Portuguese approached. He too prostrated before Usenge, a smile on his face.

"I take it you have enough captives to serve your needs?" Usenge asked.

"More than enough," Joham replied. "I will return to my ships with these. My second in command is bringing the others."

"It seems your cannons did what was required of them."

"Yes, it seems they did, great Usenge."

Usenge held out his hand. A servant placed a leather pouch in his palm. Joham's eyes gleamed. Usenge tossed the pouch to Joham and he caught it with both hands. His fingers trembled as he opened the pouch. Inside was a mix of gold and jewels.

"Thank you Great Usenge! Thank you!"

"Take you captives," Usenge said. "I expect you to return to me once you've dealt with them."

"I will," Joham replied.

Joham prostrated again before leaving Usenge's presence.

"Prepare the city," he said to his warriors. "Changa and the others will be here soon."

He rose from his stool then strode to his hut. Caungula lay on his back on a blood-crusted granite slab, tugging at the leather straps that held him in place. Usenge circled the table, his arms folded behind his back as he studied the struggling man.

"Those of lineage make the best Tukuju," he said. "Their spirits are strong and their minds the most malleable. You would think it would be different from those use to giving orders. But I have found it not to be true."

An acolyte crouched over a simmering pot, whispering words that seemed incoherent but were filled with powerful meanings. He inserted a long needle into the concoction, his chanting rising in volume as he bathed the needle. Usenge held out his hand as he passed the acolyte. The man gave the thin metal shaft to the sorcerer.

"It's not all bad," Usenge said. "For you will see Changa again. Unfortunately, you will not recognize him."

Usenge stabbed the needle into Caungula's head through his nostril. Caungula jerked, his mouth opening as if he was about to cry out but then his jaws went slack as his eyes blanked. Usenge twisted the needle back and forth then slowly pulled it from Caungula's face. The needle was covered with a thick gray mass. Usenge gave the needle back to the acolyte; he submerged it into the solution then handed it back to the sorcerer.

"What was once yours, now belongs to me," Usenge whispered. He stuck the needle into Caungula's nostril again. This time when he withdrew the lance it was clean. Caungula's mouth closed and life returned to his eyes. But there was a difference in his gaze. It was a look of one waiting to be commanded.

"Untie him," Usenge ordered.

The acolytes untied Caungula then stepped away.

"Rise," Usenge said.

Caungula sat up on the stone, staring into the distance.

"Who do you serve?" Usenge asked.

"Usenge," Caungula replied.

"Who do you hate?"

"Changa Diop."

"Do you remember his face?"

"Yeeessssss."

Usenge grinned. "When you see him, you will kill him and bring his head to me."

Caungula turned his head to face Usenge.

"Yeeeessssssss."

-12-

Changa's army numbered in the hundreds. The word of their advance preceded them and warriors waited at every village and city to join them. Usenge's rule had robbed many of hope, but now that Changa had returned new anticipation burned bright in their hearts. The army marched hard throughout the day, taking their rest in the evenings. Changa met with the new arrivals and their leaders, quickly deciding on the order of command as the force expanded. It was essential that they be organized when they confronted Usenge and his minions. Whatever the sorcerer threw at them would be easier to face with a disciplined army rather than an unruly mass.

Another day of marching brought them within striking distance of Usenge's city. As Changa suspected the sorcerer knew they were coming. The land before the city had been abandoned and burned in hope of depriving Changa's army of any provisions. Changa and his leaders had anticipated Usenge's tactic and taken the pains to set up a supply line that extended beyond Cilombo. They knew their warriors would at least be well fed before battle.

The night before the attack the warriors built a large bonfire in the center of the encampment. The flames blazed bright, illuminating the drummers and dancers celebrating before the battle. Changa sat with the leaders, enjoying a fine meal offered by the local villagers. As they ate the elders presented themselves, showering praise on Changa's and the others. Changa accepted the accolades graciously while a tempest churned in his heart. So many had come to see him defeat Usenge but despite his victories against the sorcerer's minions he still held doubt. He was deep into his contemplations when a commotion in the distance drew the attention of him and the others. Among the shouts and ululations one word became clear, Caungula.

Changa was on his feet and running in the direction of the chaos before the others could join him. The crowd parted and Changa's cousin, Caungula stood before him. It had been many years since Changa seen his cousin but his face was clearly recognizable.

"Caungula!" Changa said. "I'm so happy to see you after so many years."

"Changa," his cousin replied.

It was the way Caungula said Changa's name that warned him. Changa was already stepping away when Caungula pulled his sword and attacked. Changa dodged a swing at his throat, then sidestepped a thrust aimed for his heart. Two warriors nearby rush in to attack but were quickly cut down by Caungula. Sadness and anger gripped Changa as he circled with his cousin. Usenge had corrupted his mind and sent him to kill Changa.

Other warriors gathered, ready to attack Caungula. Changa waved them back.

"Changa, we must kill him!" Ligongo shouted. "He is no longer your cousin. He is a Tukuju!"

"No," Changa shouted.

Changa stopped, standing straight as he pushed out his chest.

"If you wish to kill me, Caungula, then do so," he said. "Your master will be proud."

Caungula hesitated. Changa smirked, knowing that some of his cousin still existed inside his mind. But then Caungula lunged, his sword once again aimed at Changa's heart. Changa waited until Caungula was fully committed before pivoting out on the ball of his left foot and dodging Caungula's thrust. He slammed his fist down on Caungula's sword hand, knocking the sword free. Before Caungula could turn Changa was directly behind him. He wrapped his cousin into a tight hold then swept his feet from under him. Caungula landed hard on his chest, the wind knocked out of him. Before he could regain his breath Changa applied pressure to the vein brining blood to Caungula's altered brain. Caungula went limp in his arms.

"Bring me your strongest ropes!" Changa called out.

Warrior scrambled away then returned with ropes. They tied Caungula's arms behind his back then bound his legs as well.

"Take him to my camp," Changa said.

Ligongo was the first to protest again.

"You can't do this Changa," he said. "Once a person has been turned into a Tukuju there is no turning back."

"No one has ever tried," Changa replied.

"You have done many amazing things Changa," Ligongo said. "But I think this is beyond you."

"I have to try," Changa answered. "Long ago Caungula and his baba saved my life. I could not save his father, but I can try to save him."

"And if you can't?"

Changa's face turned grim.

"If I can't, then I'll kill him."

Caungula's attack stole the camaraderie of the camp. The warriors separated themselves by villages, brooding about the next day. Changa could not blame them. Caungula's assault unnerved him as well. He realized now that if he could not defeat Usenge death might escape them, that he might be trapped inside his own body serving the one whom he hated most. He would be a grotesque living trophy for the sorcerer to display to his enemies. Changa stood, looking into the starlit sky. His mouth opened but then he stopped. He would not pray, nor would he speak to the ancestors. He had traveled to many lands and faced many dangers, human and otherwise. Tomorrow when he reached Usenge's city he would face his final challenge. Whether he lived or died was in his own hands. He would not have it any other way.

Sleep was brief for Changa yet he felt energized. He woke up from his cot, donning his armor and weapons. As soon as he was ready he stirred Ligongo. The warrior sprang from his cot, eyes alert. He relaxed as he recognized Changa.

"Wake the warriors," Changa said. "It's time."

Ligongo nodded then sprinted from their tent. The camp awakened with purpose, warriors arming themselves and inspecting their cohorts. Changa sauntered to the head of the road leading to Usenge's lair, the warriors watching his every step. As he reached the lead of the army they gathered around him, the commanders joining him in a semi-circle. Changa scanned them and was pleased.

"I did not grow up among you," Changa said. "But in my heart, I am baKongo!"

The warriors rattled their spears, shields and swords in response. Shouts of his name peppered the gathering.

"I have traveled to many lands and I have seen many wondrous things, but nothing more beautiful or more wonderful than my home. Usenge's monsters have followed me every step of the way, yet they have not deterred me. That is his power; that has been my burden. But I have defeated them every time. The closer I came to home, the stronger they became, yet I still killed them. Now I have one more beast to slay and I will be free, the creature that calls itself Usenge. When he is dead you will be free. Our families will be free!"

The men were shouting now, shaking their weapons in the air. Changa waited until the din subsided.

"I do not need to tell you how to fight this day," Changa continued. "You are all warriors. Some of you have fought against each other. But today we fight as one. It is simple. We win, or we die. I don't know about you, but I expect to win."

The warriors cheered as Changa turned his back and marched away. The commanders broke away, joining their respective units. Only Ligongo remained by his side.

"Will we win, Changa?" he asked.

"I don't know," Changa replied. "But whether we win or lose, we will be free."

Changa smirked at Ligongo then began to run.

Changa's army ran through the bush, spreading out into a long line. They sped through the villages, paying no notice to the inhabitants as they hurried out of the way or hid in their homes. Some grabbed their weapons and joined them. By the time they reached the borders of the city the army had almost doubled in size, but Changa found no comfort in such numbers. He could not depend on people caught up in the moment; as soon as Usenge's force struck they would scatter in fear. Their hope rested in the hands of the warriors gathered before Cilombo, those who had determined to win the day.

They broke into the clearing to see Usenge's forces standing in formation. His warriors stood bare-chested, their torsos covered by beaded necklaces of gris-gris. Bark cloth pagnes fell from their waists to their calves, their feet bare. The warriors brandished spears, swords and throwing knives, yelling at Changa's forces as they advanced. Usenge loomed behind them, staring expressionless though his eye slits. Changa felt the nyanga's eyes on him; his skin warmed as anger rose inside. But he would not let his emotions control him. At least not yet.

Usenge raised his left hand. Archers emerged from the ranks, aiming their short bows loaded with poisoned arrows at Changa's army. They turned their heads toward the sorcerer in unison anticipating his signal. Usenge waited until Changa's forces were within range then dropped his hand in a chopping motion. The archers snapped their heads about then loosed a volley of arrows. Changa's warriors twisted their bodies, most of them dodging the poisoned projectiles. The hapless ones fell to the ground as the arrows pierced their flesh, writhing in pain as the nefarious potions burned through their bodies.

"Kill them all!" Usenge shouted, his voice booming over the battle cries of the baKongo. Both sides flung spears and throwing knives before crashing into each other amid a cacophony of clashing weapons and smashing shields. Changa beat his way through the throng, his eyes focused on Usenge. The sorcerer stood motionless, watching the battle with impassive eyes. Changa fought his way toward him, his mind distracted. He realized his concern as he neared the sorcerer. Where were the Tukuju?

His question was answered by a death-like cry that shook him still. Hundreds of Tukuju emerged from behind Changa's army, swinging their giant swords like scythes into a harvest of flesh. Ligongo rushed to the rear, attempting to organize some type of resistance but it was too late. Changa wanted to join him but his only hope to preventing a full-scale massacre was to reach and kill Usenge. The Tukuju had arrived but the sorcerer remained unprotected. If he was to end it, it had to be now.

A warrior jumped before him and Changa punched him from view. Two more blocked his way and he killed both almost as fast as they appeared. More of Usenge's guards attempted to block his way but Changa would not be denied. This would end today.

The attacks diminished and Changa dared to look about. They were losing. Usenge's forces had caught them by surprise and the Kongo warriors were confused and afraid. Changa fought his way through the chaos, ignoring the carnage taking place around him. There only one thing he could so to stop it; kill Usenge.

The Kongo warriors before him let out a collective cry then dispersed in every direction, revealing a throng of half-dead warriors trotting toward him. Apparently Usenge kept a few of his minions as a precaution. Changa felt Kintu's Gift rise within him as he charged toward Usenge's vanguard, sword in one hand, throwing knife in the other. He decapitated the first warrior to reach him then squatted low, causing the sword swing of the second warrior to pass over him. He rammed his shoulder into the being's gut then stood up, tossing it over him. His arms became a blur as he hacked and cut the other beings, ignoring the minor wounds inflicted by their blades. Moments later he was surrounded by the carcasses of men experiencing their second and final death. Changa took a glance at his work then looked into the wooden face and burning eyes of Usenge. The sorcerer stared back, the expression on his mask changing as if made of flesh. He carried a wooden shield on his left arm, but it was the weapon in his right hand that captured Changa's attention and anger. It was the same sword Usenge used to kill his father. Usenge glanced at the sword then looked back to Changa.

"As it was for the father, so it shall be for the son," he said.

Changa attacked. Usenge raised his shield to block Changa's blade; Changa's sword struck the shield and it shattered into splinters. The sorcerer managed to raise his sword, blocking Changa's vicious backswing. The force almost spun the sorcerer around, turning his away to leave his back exposed. Changa's blade barely penetrated Usenge's skin before he turned and knocked Changa's blade away. They circled, Changa barely controlling his rage.

"You are stronger than him," Usenge said. "But still not strong enough."

Usenge came at Changa, his swordplay powerful and swift. Changa barely kept time, blocking and dodging each blow, his strength waning with each exchange. This was not happening, he thought. All the years of training, all the talisman gathered; it could not end like this. Usenge seemed to get stronger with every blow. Changa dropped his throwing knife, grasping his sword hilt with both hands. Still he could not stem the sorcerer's assault. Usenge swung at his neck and he blocked the blow, his sword flying from his tired hand. Before he could retrieve it the cold hands more Tukuju grasped his arms then forced him to his knees. He looked up into Usenge's mask.

"How did you think this would end?" the sorcerer asked. "You thought you would come and defeat me because you killed a few tebos? You were naïve, just like Mfumu. You have caused enough distractions. Time to join you father, Son of Mfumu!"

Usenge was raising his sword when one of the Tukuju holding Changa jerked then fell to the ground. Seconds later the others did the same. Usenge looked beyond Changa.

"You!" he shouted.

A barrage of war clubs pummeled the sorcerer, driving him back. Usenge attempted to stand his ground but the assault was too much. He backed away then finally turned and ran away. Fatigue, relief and shame swept over Changa and he collapsed into the dirt. He rolled onto his back to see a group of warriors draped in leopard skins standing over him. The warriors cleared, making room for a woman with a fierce expression wearing the headring of a kabaka.

"So, you are Mfumu's son," she said. "How disappointing."

She looked to her warriors.

"Pick him up," she said. "Let's see if the ancestors are kinder to him than Usenge."

Changa did not resist as the warriors lifted him from the ground. So many years of planning and preparation, all of it for nothing. Changa succumbed to his wounds as the warriors carried him from the battlefield.

- 1 3 -

Changa awoke to the smell of palm oil and incense. He sat up from the cot on which he lay then looked about the strange house in which he rested. He spotted movement in the corner of his eye then sprang to his feet, reaching for weapons that were not there. The source of the sound, a young woman draped in leather armor covered by a swath of leopard skin smiled slightly then exited the house without speaking. Changa began to follow but decided not to. He had no idea what was on the other side of the door and having no weapons, had no way of defending himself. He would wait for whatever came.

As he waited a cloud of despondence settled on his mind. He'd finally met Usenge face to face and he had failed. The sorcerer was moments from taking his life as he did his father before the intervention, from whom or what he did not know. It did not matter. Since fleeing for his life all those years ago one thought kept him alive and sustained him throughout any dangers he faced. All the journeys, all the training served one purpose. And in the end, it wasn't enough.

The door to the house opened and the warrior re-entered. She was not alone. Another woman followed flanked by two men dressed in the leopard garments. The woman wore them as well. A thin golden band encircled her curled hair, her handsome face graced with a stern stare. One of the men placed a stool before Changa and the woman sat. It took Changa moment to recognize her as the woman who loomed over him after Usenge was driven away. The kabaka studied Changa for a moment as a grin formed on her face.

"I am Vatukemba," the woman said.

Changa nodded. "I think you know who I am."

"I do," Vatukemba replied.

"Thank you…for saving me," Changa said.

Vatukemba nodded. "We saved many of your warriors as well."

"I thank you for them also. Did Ligongo survive?"

Vatukemba frowned. "Unfortunately, yes. The fool."

"He is not to blame for what happened," Changa replied. "The blame rests on my shoulders. I thought we were strong enough. I thought I was strong enough."

"You were not, and Ligongo should have known," Vatukemba said. "They were imbeciles, all of them. They were not ready and neither were you."

"You are the one they told me about," Changa said. "The one who left Kongo."

Vatukemba laughed. "They still hold on to old grudges. They were foolish then. They did not listen to the spirit talkers."

"Spirit talkers?" Changa was confused. "If you were not in Kongo, how did you know of our plans to attack Usenge?"

"Because I told her."

Kaihemba entered the house, a wide grin on his face. Changa was relieved to see the old man was still alive.

"Kaihemba came to us and told us of your plans," Vatukemba said.

"Yes, I did!" Kaihemba said. "At first she refused to come. It took much convincing and many conversations with the ancestors to finally convince her."

Changa's eyes narrowed. "So, it was not your choice to come?"

Vatukemba met his gaze. "No. You are not the only person entitled to rule Kongo. You see, we are cousins. I have your father's blood running through my veins as well. If you were dead, the ancestors would favor me and give me the power to defeat Usenge."

Changa crossed his arms across his chest. This was a dangerous situation for him. But it did not matter. He had failed his life's ambition. Something else came to his mind of the moment before Vatukemba saved him.

"Usenge knew you," he said.

Vatukemba frowned. "Yes, he does. Although he does not fear me as he did then."

"Fear you?" Changa was dumbfounded.

"The word of your baba's death spread quickly throughout Kongo," Vatukemba said. "We were all prepared to rally around you, but then Usenge attacked Cilombo and you were presumed dead. Usenge's attack sparked panic among anyone of lineage. They thought he would hunt them down like he did you, so they all fled."

"But you did not," Changa said.

"No. My family did. My father was your uncle and he was more afraid than most. But I was not. I was a warrior, and I saw an opportunity. While Usenge expected everyone to run away from him, I decided to run to him."

"A good plan, if you were his equal," Changa said.

"I thought it was and I thought I was," Vatukemba replied. "I made my way to Alongi unmolested. Most people thought I served Usenge and avoided me. What other reason would anyone journey to Alongi."

MILTON J DAVIS

Vatukemba fell silent, a smile coming to her face.

"It almost worked," she continued. "I fell in with a group of warriors Usenge had summoned from beyond Kongo. We arrived as others did. A great celebration was taking place. Usenge sat at the center, his face full of pride. This was before he took the mask. I danced with the others, slowly working my way closer to him. I only needed to get within throwing range. Once I did I snatched a club from my sash and threw it as hard as I could. He saw the club but there was nothing he could do."

"But you missed your mark," Changa said.

"I do not miss," Vatukemba said. "A warrior danced into the way. The club struck his head and killed him. Usenge was on his feet shouted and pointing toward me as the fool fell. I was halfway out of the celebration when the others realized what had occurred. The chased me for weeks. They did not stop until I was far beyond Kongo."

"If you had killed him you would be kabaka," Changa said. "If you had let me die you would be next in line to rule."

Vatukemba nodded.

"Yet you did not let me die nor did you finish the job yourself."

Vatukemba glanced at Kaihemba. "I would never let anyone die at the hands of Usenge, no matter how I felt about them. No one deserves the wrath of that monster, especially the son of Mfumu. As far as not killing you myself, the spirit talker convinced me not to."

Changa looked to Kaihemba. "So, I have you to thank for my life."

"Yes, you do!" Kaihemba replied. "It is true that if you died Vatukemba could receive the ancestors blessing to challenge Usenge. But killing Usenge is your destiny if you are worthy. The ancestors have told me as much."

"You said could," Changa said. "The ancestors' blessing is not sure?"

Vatukemba laughed again. "In order to receive their blessing, you must pass their initiation. Only then will you have a chance to defeat Usenge."

Changa felt new hope.

"Where does this initiation take place?" he asked.

"Far from here," Vatukemba replied. "It will take time to organize a trek and even longer to reach the ancestors' tree."

"What must I do?"

Vatukemba rubbed her chin. "You can do nothing. I will send word out. Once the proper people have gathered we will begin our journey. But you must understand we are making a great sacrifice."

"How so?" Changa asked.

"Usenge is coming for you. He will march across the Kongo destroying everything in his path to find you. Many will die as we determine if the ancestors favor you."

"What can we do to prevent him?"

Vatukemba frowned. "I'm not sure. Your army is decimated and my army is not large enough. The only thing we can do is appease him."

"How will we do that?"

"We will give him what he's always wanted," Vatukemba said. "We will give him Kongo."

"No!" Changa said. "We can't ask these people to surrender to him."

"Do you have another suggestion?" Vatukemba asked. "Besides, it will only be temporary. You are the son of Mfumu. If what the spirit talker says is true, the ancestors will give you their blessing and you will return and defeat Usenge."

The doubt that Changa felt earlier resurfaced.
"And if I'm not?"

"Then we would have saved the sorcerer the trouble," Vatukemba said. "We would have given him what he would have eventually gained."

"I will not fail," Changa said. "Not this time."

"That is not yours to claim," Vatukemba replied. "The ancestors will decide."

Vatukemba stood.

"Rest Changa," she said. "The days ahead will be arduous. I have much to plan. I will send for you when we are ready."

Vatukemba exited the house, her warriors following. Changa sat on the bed, shaking his head.

"You must keep your strength," Kaihemba said.

Changa looked up at the old man and smiled.

"You're still here? I thought you would be with Vatukemba. She seems to be the only person who trusts your word other than me."

"She is close to the ancestors," Kaihemba said. "As are you."

Changa laughed. "I have been from the Kongo to Mombasa. I've sailed from the shores of Sofala to the harbors of the Middle Kingdom. I've trekked from the mountains of the Mongols to the peaks of Axum. I've seen the mosques of Timbuktu and drifted in the waters of the Joliba. And not one time during any of these safaris have I heard the voices of the ancestors."

"Because you refused to listen," Kaihemba said.

Kaihemba sat on the floor before Changa then crossed his legs.

"Sometimes I curse the blessing given to me," he said. "Do you think I do not know how people treat me because of it? Yes, I act as if though the insults don't affect me, but they do. Because I choose to be the voice of the ancestors I gave up the chance to have a wife and children that would remember my name and perpetuate my soul. My path is a solitary path, and sometimes it can be lonely."

"I'm sorry," Changa said.

"There's no need for you to apologize, Son of Mfumu. This is not your doing. I have chosen to speak for the ancestors and so I have. So, do as Vatukemba said. Rest. You must be prepared for what is to come."

Kaihemba stood then left. Changa lay down and tried to rest but there was too much on his mind. He left the house as well and wandered Vatukemba's city. The wide streets and wooden structures resembled those of the Kongo. There were three markets, with the main market near Vatukemba's palace. The home of the leopard kabaka was modest compared to those he had seen among his people, the only indication of its status the guards stationed at the compound entrance. It was a prosperous city and most likely a prosperous realm, one that any kabaka would be proud.

Changa found his warriors huddled together at the city outskirts. They looked up to him as he approached with a mixture of emotions, the most dominate being shame. They had lost a battle that they hoped would rid them of Usenge once and for all, and they were tending their wounds in the city of a woman they despised. He spotted the leaders sitting together around a small fire. Ligongo was the first to see him and stood immediately. He made his way to Changa, the others following. The men met then hugged.

"I'm glad to see you are well," Ligongo said.

"I'm happy you are well too," Changa replied.

Ligongo's weak smile faded.

"We failed you," he said.

"We all failed," Changa replied. "Usenge was stronger than we anticipated. We were overconfident, which opened us to the Tukuju ambush. And I was not strong enough to kill Usenge."

Ligongo hesitated before speaking.

"What do we do now?" he asked.

"Vatukemba has a plan."

Ligongo spat. "We will listen to her?"

"You have an extremely short memory," Changa said. "If not for Vatukemba we would all be dead or wishing we were. Despite all you said about her she came to fight, even though we did not summon her."

"How did she discover our plans?"

"Kaihemba told her."

"She listened to the crazy man?"

"It's good she did," Changa said. "As I said, Vatukemba has a plan."

"I won't go along with it!"

"You may not; that is your choice. But I will."

"Changa, this is madness!" Ligongo gripped his shoulders. "We are still reeling from this set back. All we need is a few days to recover then we can gather to devise another strategy."

"There is no other strategy," Changa said. "I will go with Vatukemba to the ancestors' tree and submit to the initiation."

Changa and the others lingered in Vatukemba's city while preparations for the journey to the Ancestors Tree were made. Changa and Vatukemba barely spoke during that time, the tension between them obvious to everyone. The Leopard Warriors did not hide their feelings toward him, but none dared approach. They had heard from the others how he handled the Tukuju single-handedly, a feat that even their leopard mother could not claim. It was a relief when the preparations were done and the journey began. Changa and his warriors were healed and ready to depart; Vatukemba and her warriors would accompany them as well. It would not be an ideal situation but at least they would be away from the eyes and mouths of the city.

Changa and Ligongo traveled with Vatukemba and Kaihemba. Vatukemba's children accompanied them as well, including a warrior that was no relation to the kabaka yet apparently well regarded. While Vatukemba's children kept their distance, the woman seemed to constantly drift near Changa and the others. At the end of their second day the woman dropped all pretenses. Changa was sitting before a fire with Ligongo when the woman approached and sat beside him.

"I am Kifunji," she said.

"Go away, leopard woman," Ligongo said.

"No," Changa countered. He offered his bowl to her. The woman looked surprised then shook her head.

"No, thank you," she said. "I have eaten."

Ligongo huffed then left the fire to join the others. Kifunji frowned as she watched him walk away then turned her attention back to Changa.

"I am newly initiated to the Children," she said.

"Congratulations," Changa replied.

"The Mother thinks very highly of me."

"Your opinion may be tarnished by sitting with me," Changa replied.

"I have earned my place," she said. "I fear no one's opinion."

Kifunji picked up a stick and poked at the fire.

"What do you plan to do if the ancestors favor you?"

"I will kill Usenge," Changa said.

"And after that?"

Changa looked at Kifunji. He'd never been asked that question before. He'd never asked the question of himself.

"I don't know."

"If you defeat him you will have earned the right reclaim your father's legacy."

"Yes, I guess that would be true."

"So, will you?"

Changa smirked. "Why are you asking all these questions? Did Vatukemba send you?"

Kifunji smiled. "She did. But I ask these questions for myself as well."

Changa's amusement turned to curiosity.

"So why is my future a concern to you?"

Kifunji's expression turned serious.

"Do you have a wife, Changa?"

The question caught Changa off guard.

"Ah, no," he answered.

"But you have a woman. I can see it in your eyes."

"Yes. There is someone."

"Is she here?"

Changa's mood turned somber. "No, she is far from here."

"If you stay in Kongo, you will need a wife. I will be your wife."

Changa's eyes went wide. "What?"

Kifunji's expression remained serious. "I will be your wife. A man like you will need a strong companion. I'm capable and I am young, which mean I will bear many warriors. Also, a marriage between us will form an alliance with Vatukemba. Since I am one of her children I would serve you both."

"Marriage and alliances are the last thing on my mind, Kifunji," Changa replied.

"You cannot deny that I am capable. I am also attractive, don't you think?"

Changa sighed. "Kifunji, your conversation has become tiring. I'd like to enjoy the rest of my evening in peace."

Kifunji stood. "I understand. Consider my words, Changa. It would be a prosperous union for everyone." Kifunji walked away with a confident stride. Changa watched her for a moment before returning to his own thoughts. Ligongo returned moments later.

"What did the leopard woman want?" he asked.

"She wants to marry me," Changa replied.

"What?!? These people are crazy! We would do best to return to Kongo and raise a new army."

"If we go back to Kongo we will suffer the same fate," Changa said. "I cannot defeat Usenge, and if I can't stop him we cannot win."

"I asked you before and I'll ask you again. Do you believe Vatukemba and that nonsense?"

Changa shrugged. "I have no choice."

"We can go back and consult our sorcerers to see if there is another way."

"We can. But now I will follow Vatukemba to this tree to see if what she says is true."

Ligongo grasped Changa's shoulders and turned him to face him.

"Changa, please reconsider. For all we know she may be leading you into a trap."

Changa smirked. "That may be true, but what other choice do I have?"

Changa patted Ligongo's shoulder.

"You don't have to come with me," Changa said. "I began this journey alone and I will end it alone. If you feel this is a trap, don't endanger your life and the lives of your warriors. This is my safari."

"We will follow you, Changa," Ligongo said. "Either we will see the ancestors grant you the power to kill Usenge or we will kill Vatukemba and her leopards for lying to us."

"Let's hope it doesn't come to that," Changa replied.

Changa spent another restless night. He thought his mind would be focused on the coming events, but instead he thought of Panya. He recalled his last night with her before he set off on this safari and how confident she was in his success. It was she who convinced him to take this journey when he had seriously considered giving it up.

"You still have fear inside you," she said. "You cannot be the man I need you to be until you rid yourself of it."

Her words were true. Despite leading the army against Usenge and fighting him, the terror of a boy watching his father murdered rested deep inside, refusing to let go of his heart. He realized that his fear was the reason he had traveled so far for so long, thinking of so many reasons not to return home. Now he was where he dreaded to be, confronting the man who planted such a weakness inside him. His mind drifted back to Panya, her beautiful smile, her comforting embrace, her firm and passionate body. Why did it take him so long to notice her? It was an irrelevant question. He loved her now, and she loved him.

The morning came and the travelers continued their journey. They finally emerged from Vatukemba's valley onto a wide plateau covered with rolling hills interspersed with grasslands. Wildlife was abundant; they supplemented their provision with wild game. There was little conversation between the groups, although Kifunji made sure Changa noticed her on a daily basis. On the third night of their journey the leopard warriors gathered around the fire, beating their drums and singing a song well known to them all. Changa and his warriors gathered on the outside of the circle.

"What new madness is this?" Ligongo asked.

Changa smiled. "One I know well."

Two warriors entered the circle, bare-chested and wearing leopard printed loincloths. They danced to the rhythm for a few moments then launched into a dizzying display of acrobatics. Then they fought in the style of Kongo, evading each other's blows with grace as they attempted to defeat each other. A solid blow ended the fight, and the defeated leopard was replaced. The fighting continued until one person stood in the circle, Kifunji.

She danced alone as the others cheered her victory. But Changa knew it was not over. There was a high-pitched scream and Vatukemba appeared, her face covered with her leopard mask. There was no acrobatics between these two. They fought immediately. Kifunji was skilled, but it was obvious Vatukemba toyed with her, much to Kifunji's frustration. Vatukemba finally brought the competition to an end, landing a kick to Kifunji's chest that sent her sprawling onto the ground. Kifunji stood then prostrated before Vatukemba, frustration clear on her face. Vatukemba touched her head and the woman rose from the dirt. She glanced toward Changa, clearly embarrassed.

The drummers and singers were about to disperse when Vatukemba raised her hand.

"Wait," she said. Her eyes met Changa's.

"Son of Mfumu, shall we play?" she asked.

"This is not necessary," Changa said.

Vatukemba's eyes narrowed. "Yes. It is."

Ligongo's warriors immediately took up a chant which was answered by Vatukemba's leopards. Hundreds of expectant eyes rested on Changa. This was a waste of time, a situation that threatened more harm than good. He would have to be careful.

Changa began stripping off his clothing and both sides let out loud roar. That roar became gasps as he revealed his muscled scarred torso. He sauntered into the circle, halting before Vatukemba.

"Impressive," she said.

"Let's get on with it," Changa replied.

Vatukemba grinned. "I promised Kifunji I would not hurt the important parts."

"That wasn't your promise to make," he said.

Vatukemba answered with a swirling kick that barely missed Changa's jaw. She flowed into a pair of hand strikes which Changa dodged then followed them with a foot sweep that Changa hopped over. Changa could barely remember his *ngolo* training so he would not embarrass himself attempting to fight Vatukemba in such a way. Instead he fell back onto his skills from the pit, a style that held no glamour but was nonetheless effective.

Vatukemba kept up her attack, blows and kicks coming from all angles. Any person not familiar with *ngolo* would have been pummeled to submission long ago. Such was the speed and power of the Leopard Mama. Changa continued blocking and dodging, waiting for his moment. It came as he knew it would; Vatukemba had exhausted her attacks and hesitate for one second before beginning another flurry. It was all Changa needed. He launched his own attack and Vatukemba immediately went on the defensive. Amid his focus he couldn't help but admire her style. She moved effortlessly, like hummingbird flittering through the bush. Changa's chance came as the Leopard Mama rose on one arm to deliver double kick. Changa evaded then kicked Vatukemba's arm. She fell, striking her shoulder on the ground. Before he could move in she rolled back onto her feet, rubbing her shoulder. She launched another series of attacks, Changa evading the best he could. An open palm slipped by his defenses and smacked his chin; as he recovered Vatukemba landed a kick to his chest that knocked him onto his back. Changa executed a back roll that took him out of the path of Vatukemba's stomp and back onto his feet.

"Enough of this!" he said.

He jumped forward, jamming Vatukemba's kick. Vatukemba punched at his throat but Changa caught her wrist and twisted. The Leopard Mama grimaced as the pressure forced her to turn her back to Changa. Changa evaded her backwards head strike then wrapped his arms around her neck, applying pressure in the proper place. Vatukemba struggles subsided and moments later she fell limp in his arms. The leopard warriors cried out and rushed the circle; Ligongo and his men did the same. Changa paid neither side any attention as he eased the unconscious woman to the ground. As the groups were about to clash he struck Vatukemba hard on her back. Her eyes opened; she looked about dazed for a moment then raised her hand. The leopard warriors halted. Changa looked at Ligongo and his warriors and they did the same.

Changa stood then lifted Vatukemba to her feet. The Leopard Mama turned to face him, removing her mask as she did so to reveal her admiring expression.

"It's been a very long time since I've been de-feated in the circle," she said.

"It happens to the best of us," Changa replied. "It was a long time before I was victorious in the circle."

"Maybe you are who Kaihemba says you are."

"We will know soon," Changa said.

"Yes, we will," Vatukemba replied.

Vatukemba nodded slightly then walked away. Her children followed, many of them glancing back at Changa with various expressions. Kifunji looked the longest, a smile on her face. Changa laughed.

"You were magnificent!" Ligongo said.

Changa dusted off then picked up his garments as he strolled back to his campfire.

"I wouldn't say that," he replied. "She's an excellent fighter. I see why they follow her."

"They will follow you now," Ligongo said.

"We'll see."

That night at the fire it was not Kifunji who visited him. Vatukemba emerged from the darkness, accompanied by two women and one man, each bearing a torch. Their similar faces revealed them to be Vatukemba's children. None of them seemed pleased with him. Vatukemba sat beside Changa but the children remained standing.

"Tomorrow will be like nothing you've ever experienced," Vatukemba said.

"You have no idea what I have experienced," Changa replied.

"That is true. But I have an idea that this will be a new experience for you."

"Have you been tested?" Changa asked.

Vatukemba looked away. "Yes. Twice."

"And both times the ancestors have rejected you."

Vatukemba looked into the fire. "Yes."

Changa said nothing. He could imagine the shame Vatukemba felt. It would be the same for him if they did not accept him.

"It took me weeks to recover, not only mentally but physically."

"There will be a physical challenge?"

"Yes and no."

"I don't understand."

Vatukemba look into Changa's eyes. "Your test will be different from mine. Both of my tests were different from each other. The ancestors will tap into your worst fears to break you. There is nothing you can hide from them. You must be prepared for anything and everything."

"I will be ready," Changa said. "I have no choice."

Vatukemba smiled. "That is good to hear, Changa. You are not boastful or overconfident."

"I have dealt with the spirits before," Changa replied. "I know how unpredictable they can be."

"I wish you well tomorrow, Son of Mfumu," Vatukemba said as she stood.

"Even if it means you cannot lead the baKongo?" Changa asked.

"If the ancestors choose you then I will follow you," Vatukemba said. "Who am I to stand against their wisdom?"

"Thank you," Changa said. "You are an honorable leader. I see why your warriors love you."

Vatukemba grinned. "They have no choice. I am their mother. Their love is unconditional."

Vatukemba and her children left Changa alone at the fire. Changa slept soon afterwards, his dreams filled with old memories and old friends.

- 1 4 -

Two weeks had passed since Usenge's confrontation with Changa and the sorcerer's anger still had not settled. The inhabitants of Alongi hid in fear as he unleashed his wrath on all around him. Only the mindless Tukuju dared to be close to him, and many of them were destroyed in his rampages. More than once he'd considered killing Changa's mother and sisters in revenge, but stopped just short. They would welcome the escape; his worse torture for them was to keep them alive. So he spared them, although he managed to make their existence more miserable by sending them to a sparse hut at the edge of his realm.

When he had finally settled enough to think with reason he sent for his commanders. The warriors stood before him, each doing well to mask their nervousness. The Portuguese came as well. Joham's fear was evident in his paler than normal complexion and the sweat that dripped from under his ridiculous hat like wet season rain. It was he that Usenge called upon first.

"When first you returned with your captives I thought you had served me well," Usenge said. "Yet my enemies came upon me with a great army. How was that possible?"

Joham cleared his throat before answering.

"Great Usenge, I did exactly as you ordered me to do. I accompanied your men to Cilombo and used our cannon against your enemies with great effect. The city fell and we gathered prisoners. How was I to know that there were others?"

"You were impatient!" Usenge shouted. "You should have known my enemies would gather once they knew Changa had returned and the obvious place for them to convene would be Cilombo. That is why I sent you there."

"Great Usenge, how…"

"Silence!" Usenge rushed from his stood then wrapped his hand around Joham's neck. He choked the man as he lifted him from the ground.

"I know what you seek, Portuguese," he said. "You are just the beginning of a tide, a trickle that will become a torrent. I humor you because for now you serve my purpose. When I attain what I seek you and your king will be like a fly on an elephant's ass to me."

He let go of Joham and he fell to the ground.

"My spies tell me the warriors have abandoned their villages and cities," Usenge said as he sauntered back to his stool. "I want you to take you men out and raid them all. I want you to gather all the people, women, children, young and old. I want you to take them to your ships and do whatever you like to them. That will be their punishment for standing against me."

Joham massaged his neck before speaking with a strained voice.

"Great Usenge, I don't have enough ships to do as you ask."

"Must I tell you everything? There are plenty of trees near your harbor. Build them. You will have plenty of labor to help you."

"Yes, I will," Joham said.

"Leave me."

Joham took off his hat and bowed deeply. He signaled his men and they hurried away from the circle.

"Kandimba!"

The masked warrior appeared by Usenge's side.

"Are the warriors ready?"

"Yes, Great Usenge."

"Good. We will depart tomorrow."

"Great Usenge, do you think the Portuguese will be able to clear the villages?"

Usenge shrugged. "It doesn't matter. The time has come for all things to be settled. Changa will come again and this time there will be no one to save him. He travels to the Ancestor Tree to gain their blessings but it does not matter. I have my own blessings to receive."

The circle dispersed, leaving Usenge alone. He sat on his stool until the sun had descended below the trees. The darkness surrounded him, but it was not an ordinary void. He could feel it touch his skin and he shivered in anticipation. Moments later a small gorilla emerged from the bush, its eyes glowing like amber fire.

"You are summoned," the beast said, its voice seeming to come from a source beyond its body.

Usenge stood then followed the acolyte of the Ndoki into the dense woods. Neither needed light to find their destination; the journey was etched in their minds by spiritual means. The branches that brushed his arms, mask and torso gave way to emptiness; the mud and dirt beneath his feet slowly transformed into gravel then rock. They climbed, at first a gentle slope then eventually a vertical wall. Usenge's fingers slipped into groves created centuries before by others that took the fateful climb. Finally, he reached the summit of the stone mountain. The acolyte had long disappeared. Sitting before him were the Ndoki, their faces solemn.

"You have done all that we asked," they said in unison. "Except one thing."

Usenge began to respond but felt his throat constrict.

"We need no answer, for we know it is impossible for you to do. In your present form."

The Ndoki lunged for him, dragging him to the ground. Usenge did not resist; instead he smiled in anticipation. They held his arms in place as one of them opened his mouth then shoved a concoction of leaves and something Usenge did not recognize. He choked and attempted to spit the vile elixir out in reflex but the Ndoki clamped his mouth shut and massaged his throat until he swallowed it. Fire burned inside him and fear flooded his mind.

"What have you done to me!" he shouted.

"We have given you what you wished for," they said. "You will see."

Usenge thrashed involuntarily, his arms and legs flailing as the elixir spread into every part of his being. Screams burst from his throat, tearing through the otherwise silent scene. Despite the pain, he could feel his body changing.

The convulsions eventually subsided. Usenge lay still for a moment then sat up. When he studied his body, he saw that nothing had changed. He looked perplexed at the Ndoki, yet their expressions did not change as they faded into the bush.

"I don't understand," he said.

"Your transformation is not complete," they replied. "All that you have sent forth you must summon home. Gather all that is part of you. You will need it for the transformation to be complete."

"And when Changa is dead?" he asked.

"You will be among us."

- 15 -

In all his travels, Changa had never seen such a magnificent tree. The nearby baobabs were like saplings in comparison. As they neared it became difficult to see the canopy. The expansive tangle of branches and leaves resembled a green cloud overhead, diffusing the sun's light. The trunk spanned as wide as a large village. Two stone buildings sat on either side of the tree like tiny sentinels, smoke rising from their crowns. Changa looked at Vatukemba and she answered with a knowing smile.

"I know how you feel," she said. "I felt the same way when I first saw it."

"How did you find it?" he asked.

"How could you not?" she replied. "It was a few months after I escaped Usenge when I heard of its whereabouts. I had returned to Kongo once again to kill Usenge. I took rest in a small village where I was recognized by the chief. He had known my father. When I shared with him my intentions he took me to their elders. It was they who told me of it. They told me my efforts were fruitless; they said our only hope against Usenge was to call on the ancestors. Since I was the next in line for kabaka it was my duty to ask for their help. I came alone the first time with nothing to back my claim except the elders' word. My visit did not last long; the caretakers would not let me enter. I left angry, determined to prove my worth. That is when I became the Leopard Mama and built my realm."

"So, when you returned the caretakers let you enter."

Vatukemba nodded. "I thought I had done enough. But it was during my initiation that I learned I would not be chosen."

"How did you discover this?"

Vatukemba stared at Changa. "I saw you."

"You saw me?"

Vatukemba grinned. "The ancestors opened a window into the world. You were still young, but you were alive. They told me that as long as you lived the rule of Kongo would not be mine. From that day forth I hated you. I returned twice more, each time hoping for your demise. But you are tougher than you seem."

"And do you still hate me?"

Vatukemba laughed. "Not as much."

Vatukemba looked toward the tree and Changa did the same. The caretakers emerged from their temples. There were ten in all, each draped in bark cloth and wearing simple masks. They carried long spears and narrow leaf shields.

"We must wait," Vatukemba said.

The travelers stood silent as the caretakers approached. They lowered their spears and raised their shields as if to attack and Changa felt his warriors tense.

"Stand still," he ordered.

The caretakers halted within throwing range. The tallest of them kept walking forward, his spear vacillating between Vatukemba and Changa in time with his stride. The weapon finally settled on Changa. Changa did not move as the spear tip touched his chest.

"Son of Mfumu," the warrior said. "We have waited a long time for you. Come."

He lifted his spear and Changa walked toward the man. Vatukemba began to follow; the other caretakers rushed toward her, spears and shields at the ready.

"Only him," the warrior leading Changa said without turning about. "You know this, Vatukemba."

"The ancestors remember me?" she asked.

"They never forget," the caretaker replied.

Changa walked by the line of caretakers. They followed him, walking backwards with the spears lowered for a time then lifting them as they turned then followed single file behind Changa and their leader. As Changa neared the tree he saw what seemed to be a sliver in the trunk, a crack marring the otherwise smooth bark. As they came closer the crack became a gap wide enough for two men to enter. Numerous shapes were carved along the edges of the gap, symbols that Changa could not decipher. A slight breeze passed through the branches, and the clinking of metal filled his ears. He looked up to see the branches festooned with gris-gris of various kinds, a clear symbol of the spiritual strength gathered on this sacred ground.

They stood before the entrance. The tall man lowered his spear before Changa, blocking his way.

"Unburden yourself of all protection you have gathered," he said. "You will not need it here."

Changa took off Panya's beaded necklace the handed it to the tall man. He also removed Mikaeli's cross and took Zakee's jambiya from his waist belt. The tall man set the objects aside then lifted his spear. Changa took a deep breath then entered. He was instantly shrouded in darkness, yet he knew which way to go. After a few moments a faint light appeared before him. He made his way toward the light, eventually discovering a fire blazing in a small clearing. A woman sat before the fire, a pleasant smile on her aged face. She was dressed similar to the caretakers, her robe gathered about her thin waist by a red sash.

"Please sit, Son of Mfumu," she said, her voice light and comforting like a breeze.

128

Changa sat cross-legged before the woman.

"Hold out your arms then turn your palms upward," she instructed.

Changa did as he was instructed. The woman revealed a small knife.

"Don't worry," she said. "This blade will not harm you."

She grasped Changa's right arm then cut three small slits into his right forearm. She did the same with his left arm. Despite the cuts his arm barely bled.

"What is this for?" he asked.

"To release that which is inside you."

The woman revealed a small gourd. She poured a thick sweet-smelling liquid into the palm of her left hand then placed the bottle before her. After spreading the liquid on both hands, she massaged the liquid into cuts on his forearms. Changa felt a familiar stirring in his abdomen.

"Kintu's Gift," he said. "You are taking Kintu's Gift."

The woman grinned. "You no longer need it."

The stinging graduated to a sustained burning. Changa gritted his teeth as the energy migrated from his stomach then into his arms. A smoke-like mist emerged from the cuts, rising over them both then disappearing into the darkness. The woman nodded in approval, then produced a small vial.

"Drink this," she said.

Changa took the vial from the woman then removed the stopper. He looked at the woman nervously and she smiled.

"It is time," she said, "Drink."

Changa put the vial to his lips and drank. He expected some powerful sensation or overwhelming taste; instead the elixir tastes like slightly bitter water. After he finished the woman came closer.

"Lay down," she said.

Changa lay on his back, the ground soft against his muscled back.

"They are coming," she said.

The woman disappeared from his view. Moments later the world went black.

* * *

Changa opened his eye to muted sunlight. A tangle of tree branches obscured the partly clouded sky. The damp organic smell of a recent rain teased his nostrils. The ground was wet against his back so he sat up, irritated by the sensation. He lay in an open space, surrounded by bush. The air was warm and humid. It seemed a normal rainy season day, but Changa knew it was far from it. Moments ago, he was confined in the bowels of the Ancestor Tree, yet now he sat in an unknown forest.

A sharp grunt brought him to his feet. His hands went instinctively for the knives and swords that were not there. Changa studied his body; he was weaponless and naked. He had little time to contemplate his condition; the grunting grew louder, the bush before him shaking violently as something charged in his direction. Changa braced himself.

Branches burst outward and Changa's eyes went wide. The largest silverback he'd ever seen paced before him, grunting and beating his massive chest. Changa looked away, knowing that staring the beast in the eyes would be considered a challenge. He backed away, seeking to reach the bush behind him then running for safety. His back touched the vegetation, but he could not push through. The fauna pushed back, the branches like small hands against his bare back. The silverback made a false charge, crossing half the distance between then backing away and it pounded its hands on the dirt. Changa realized there would be no escape; his only way out would be through the silverback. He took a deep breath then looked into the eyes of the beast.

    The silverback charged. Changa waited until the beast was almost upon him before pivoting on his lead foot. He punched the silverback's ribs as hard as he could as he evaded the attack. To his surprise the beast staggered sideways, holding where Changa's punch landed. Changa smiled; this fight would be more even than he suspected.

    When the silverback charged again Changa did not waver. He ducked the beast's arms then rammed his shoulder into its torso. He was wrapping his arms around the beast when it slammed its elbows into Changa's back. The blow knocked Changa flat; before he could recover the silverback grasped Changa's waist, lifted him off the ground then threw him across the clearing. Changa struck the invisible barrier then fell to the ground, too stunned to rise. The silverback appeared over him, pounding him with its wrists. Changa winced as each blow sapped his strength. He yelled and kicked out at random, his heel striking the silverback's shin. The beast howled in pain then stumbled away, giving Changa enough time to stand. He ran at the silverback, ducking its maddened swing again then jumping onto its back. Changa wrapped his arms around the beast's neck, hoping to find the vein that with the right pressure would cut off the blood to its brain and render it unconscious. Before he could find it, the silverback reached over, grabbing Changa's arms then pulling him free. Again, Changa was thrown and again he struck the barrier. His body knotted in pain, he managed to regain his feet. The silverback did not charge him this time. Instead it shambled from side to side, wary of the man standing before it.

This beast was too strong despite the powers given to him, Changa surmised. He was sure this was a test from the ancestors, yet he could find no way to defeat the silverback. He decided that if he could not defeat it, he would die trying.

Man and silverback charged each other. They met in the center of the clearing. Changa's hands were quick and punishing, the silverback blows powerful and devastating. Changa felt bone break in his hands and body but he would not stop. The silverback grunted and yelled as it too was injured. Their movements became labored, stunted by the damage they both suffered. Finally, they were so wounded and exhausted they could fight no more. The silverback pounded its chest then let out a yell that seemed to fill the forest. Then it did a thing Changa had never seen a silverback do. It smiled. A knowing light emerged in its eyes then it turned and stumbled away. As it entered the bush a transformation took place. The trees surrounding Changa mutated into the shapes of countless of bodies clothed in various styles of dress. Changa could not make out any faces as he turned about to witness what was occurring. He stopped where the silverback had disappeared. The throng parted and a man stepped into the clearing. It took Changa a moment to recognize him, but when he did emotion overwhelmed him. He fell to his knees, tears coming from his eyes. The man walked up to him then knelt before him, a smile on his face.

"Baba," Changa said.

"Changa," Mfumu replied.

Father and son embraced as the ancestors surrounded them. Thousands of hands touched them, but the only hands Changa could feel were those of his father. He was a boy again, looking into his baba's face, hoping one day to be like him. Gone were the images of that fateful day. As he pulled away from his baba, the peace in his mind was a confirmation of everything he had suffered.

Son and father stood before the ancestors. Changa looked into the eyes of his lineage and his people and was humbled by their greatness.

"I stand before you with my son Changa Diop," his baba said. "He has withstood the challenge and proven his worth. Whatever happens beyond this day, you know he is worthy of our blood and our blessing."

There was a roar of approval. Mfumu held out his hand and a necklace materialized in his palm. It was a simple leather cord holding the shape of a silverback carved from ivory. Mfumu placed the necklace on Changa.

"I can defeat Usenge now," Changa said.

"If that is your destiny," Mfumu replied.

Changa was confused. "I thought that was what all this was for."

"No," baba replied. "The ancestors have pledged to support you in all that you do. It is up to you do decide what that will be."

Mfumu hugged Changa again.

"You have become the man I hoped you would be. Choose wisely and decisively. Tell your mother and sisters that I love them. A place awaits you all."

* * *

As Mfumu stepped away from Changa the scene around him faded into darkness. For a moment he felt utter peace, and then sensation reappeared. When he opened his eyes, he was in the Ancestors Tree once again, the nganga staring down at him. He reached for his neck and felt the necklace.

"It is done," the nganga said.

Changa stood then bowed to the woman.

"Go Changa Diop, Son of Mfumu," she said. "Leave this place knowing the ancestors are with you."

Changa walked away with confident strides. The ancestors told him they would support him in whatever he chose to do. His decision had been made. He emerged from the Tree in daylight. Vatukemba and the others jumped to their feet, their faces expectant. Vatukemba saw the necklace and nodded.

"The ancestors are with you," she said.

"Yes," Changa replied.

"What do you command us to do?" Ligongo asked.

Changa smiled.

-16-

The village of Bibuwa was similar to many other villages in Kongo, a collection of mud brick homes surrounded by small fields and pastures. Clusters of trees and shrubs ringed the village, gradually growing thicker the closer they approached the green mountains looming in the distance. Women and children labored in the fields as the men tended livestock and gathered wood for meals. While most kept close to the pastures, Mukendi herded his cows further away, preferring the grasses that grew near the trees. At least that is was he told his baba when asked. The truth was that he enjoyed sleeping in the shade of the camel acacias, occasionally peeking at the cattle to make sure all was well.

Normally it was an odd bellow from an errant bull that woke him, but on this day, it was the sharp snap of a breaking stick that aroused him. Mukendi stretched before opening his eyes. What he saw terrified him more that the largest simba. A mass of warriors crept toward him, some familiar, others frightening. Mukendi jumped to his feet then turned to run. He let loose one yell before the throwing club stuck his head. Mukendi fell to the ground unconscious, his cows scattering before the interlopers' onslaught.

The villagers spotted the strange men running across their fields, loud sounds like cracks of lighting emitting from their strange spears. They were followed by creatures familiar yet more terrifying. Most of the warriors had left to fight with the Son of Mfumu, thinking Usenge was their only threat. They were wrong.

Johan strolled behind his men as they swarmed the village. Those fighters that remained behind to protect the women, children and elderly were no match for the organized Portuguese and the terrible Tukuju. In minutes the people surrendered. The mercenaries ransacked every hut, dragging out those suitable for their purposes. Those they did not take they spared, much to the dislike of the Spaniard.

"I don't see why we are leaving them alive," Alfonso complained. "They are useless."

"They are human beings," Johan replied. "It is bad enough that we take their relatives. We can at least spare their lives."

"They are heathens," Alfonso replied. "Whatever they suffer is their own doing."

"Your bloodlust disturbs me," Johan said.

"This from the man who captures families to sell into slavery," the Spaniard replied.

"We both will have sins to answer to on our Judgment Day," Johan retorted. "I have a feeling I will be more content than you when that day comes."

"Enough of this talk," Alfonso said. "I'll make sure the captives are secure."

He strode away, signaling for his men to follow. Johan had second thoughts about the Spaniard. For the Portuguese mercenary this was business. He had no more ill emotions to the people of this land that he did for his brethren in Portugal or the Moors who had ruled over them for centuries. The reality was that slaves brought a high price as exotic servants to the wealthy and to the merchant farmers in the islands. If by selling them he could fill his coffers with gold he would to just that, but the local rulers held on to their precious metals more tightly that their people. Well, that was not true. The people he captured were the enemies Usenge, so in a sense he did the sorcerer a favor by ridding him of those who would oppose him. In the case of Usenge, there were many.

By the time he entered the village the people had been driven to the village center, tied and yoked. Johan inspected each person to make sure they were acceptable. It would be a long march to the coast and a long journey to Portugal so it was essential that the captives were strong enough to survive the trek to the harbor. Each person loss was a loss in profit which he couldn't afford. As he worked his way through the captives Johan decided this was his last journey to this land. He was done with the strange hold Usenge seem to have over him. Whatever the profit from this expedition, it would be enough.

After releasing those he deemed unfit to make the journey, Joham and his men drove the captives from the village. He sent the new captives to the coast with a few soldiers then continued their sweep of the surrounding lands. One by one the villages fell without a fight. By the end of two weeks the entire valley was nearly empty of people.

Johan and his men began the trek to the coast. The Tukuju abandoned them during the night, responding to Usenge's call. As they neared their base camp they encountered bodies of the captive that succumbed to the long journey. Johan frowned, more from disappointment than sadness. Each death was that much less money to be made, especially when considering those that would die during the journey north. There was nothing to be done about it. Such was the business of slavery.

As soon as he reached the camp he called his men together.

"We've gathered a rich bounty," he said. "But as you know we don't have enough ships to carry it all home. A few of you are craftsmen. I'll need your skills to build new ships. Pick the labor you need from among the slaves. Be quick about it; we have only a few more weeks with the winds in our favor. If we don't launch soon will have to feed these people for another three months.

"Or kill them," Alfonso said.

Johan glared at the Spaniard.

"You have your orders," he said to his men. "The clock begins to tick now."

-17-

Changa's army encountered the first ravaged village a week into their march. The burned huts were their first sign. As they entered the area people emerged from the surrounding bush, wailing and singing if relief. They told them what occurred, of the white men and the Tukuju that raided their home and took their loved ones. They led them to the graves of those who had fought their attackers; Changa's and the others poured libations in their honor. If there was any more reason to hate Usenge, this village was the example. They left provisions then continued their march.

The number of ruined villages increased the closer they came to Usenge's lair. Changa finally called a halt to their march then gathered his commanders. The mood was grim as he expected.

Ligongo was the first to speak.

"We must call off the attack," he said. "We have to save our loved ones before they are shipped away."

"No," Vatukemba said. "This is exactly what Usenge wants us to do. He knew this would divide us. We should press on. Once we defeat him we can rescue your families."

"It will be too late!" Ligongo shouted. "It is easy for you to sacrifice our families as your people sit safe."

"We will do both," Changa said.

Vatukemba looked at him skeptically.

"And how do you propose we do that?"

"We will send a force after the raiders," he said. "The rest of us will continue on to face Usenge."

Vatukemba shook her head. "We can't divide our forces. We need every single warrior to defeat Usenge. I know the ancestors have granted you their favor but you are still mortal. You are no use to us dead."

"I agree," Changa said. "We can't split our forces. But we can send a small group of talented warriors that should be more than enough for the Portuguese."

"Who are you talking about?" Ligongo asked.

"The Leopards," Vatukemba answered, a wide grin on her face. She threw back her head and let out a roar undistinguishable from the beast itself. In moments her warriors gathered about her, their eyes full of intent.

"What is our plan?" Vatukemba asked.

"Catch the captors," Changa said. "Once you've dealt with them come to Alongi. I think you know the way."

"Vatukemba grinned. "I do."

"What about our people?" Ligongo asked. "You will leave them unprotected?"

"We have no choice," Changa replied. "At least they will be free. They will have to fend for themselves until we return."

"If we return," Ligongo said.

Changa ignored Ligongo's sour mood. He turned to Vatukemba.

"Go," he said. "We're wasting time."

Vatukemba pulled her leopard mask over her face then ran from the circle, her warriors close behind. The last to leave was Kifunji.

"Do not die, Son of Mfumu," she said. "We have matters to discuss when I return."

"If you return," Ligongo said again.

The woman snarled at Ligongo then ran to catch up with her cohorts.

"That one will be trouble for you," Ligongo commented.

"No, she will not," Changa said. "Gather the warriors. We must hurry."

* * *

Vatukemba's scouts picked up the captives' trail not long after they left the village. The Leopards set a warrior's pace, trotting down the narrow trail single file. They stopped when needed but continued pressing. As they neared the slave party they found people in various conditions, some barely alive, others in good health but frightened. Vatukemba wanted to help them, but that would have to wait for later. Their main task was to cut off the Portuguese.

It wasn't long before they were close enough to hear the party. The sounds of grief and torment reached her ears and fueled her anger. She saw the rage among her warriors as well, but she would have to keep it under control. They would be outnumbered, so their attack would have to be sudden and precise. She stopped running, raising her hand for the others to halt. Her leaders gathered around her.

"Why are we stopping, Mama," Kifunji asked.

"We follow slowly from here," Vatukemba said. "We'll let them set up camp tonight and we will send the scouts to gather information. Once we know what we are dealing with we will plan our attack."

"We must be swift," Kifunji replied. "Changa is depending on our return."

Vatukemba frowned at Kifunji.

"Our presence or lack of it will not determine the fate of Kongo," she said. "That is why he sent us. That is in Changa's hands. We are here to free our people so that whether Changa succeeds or not, we will survive."

"But Mama, if we don't…"

"Be quiet, Kifunji!"

The woman fell silent, lowering her head respectfully.

"I am sorry Mama," she said. "It's just that…"

"I know what concerns you," Vatukemba said. "But I need you to take your head out of your loins and focus on our task. Do you understand?"

There were a few laughs and comments before Kifunji answered.

"Yes Mama. I understand."

"Good. Bakomito! Mulunda!"

The warriors appeared before Vatukemba then dropped to one knee.

"Go ahead until you find the slave party. Keep your distance and please try not to kill anyone. I need full details."

"Yes Mama!" the warriors exclaimed. They sprinted together into the bush.

The others make camp, taking the time to rest and inspect their weapons for the coming battle. Vatukemba's children surround her and prepared the evening meal. Mpata came to Vatukemba, concern on her face.

"You must do something about Kifunji," she said.

"She is nothing," Vatukemba replied. "An ambitious girl who doesn't know her place."

"Exactly. She may be trouble later."

Vatukemba laughed. "Her eyes on set on Changa. She wants to be the Kabaka's wife."

"And what of you?" Mpata said.

Vatukemba paused her club inspection to look at her daughter.

"What of me?"

"It would be a great alliance," she said. "Two powerful kingdoms joined by family and marriage."

"I have no time for politics," Vatukemba replied. "Once this is over we will return to our realm. I will have done what the ancestors have tasked me to do. If you want to form alliances, you marry him. Although you'll have to get past Kifunji first."

"I might just," Mpata replied.

"Someone should ask Changa what he thinks of all this marriage planning," Vatukemba said.

"As if he had a choice," Mpata replied.

Vatukemba chuckled as she resumed inspecting her weapons. "See to your siblings then get some rest. We battle tomorrow, and I want all my children with me when we march on Usenge."

Mpata kissed Vatukemba's cheek then left her alone at the fire. Vatukemba placed her club down, forced to think of what they had discussed. Marrying Changa would be a plus. It would extend her influence beyond her own realm and bring her back into Kongo with his favor. But then she thought of what she'd told her daughter. Changa had not spoken of any such alliances and he rebuffed Kifunji's attention. His focus was on Usenge and nothing else. But if he defeated the sorcerer such matters would need to be discussed.

There was also the possibility that he would fail despite the ancestors' will. In that event she would possibly be favored. The forces of Kongo would be gathered and she could proclaim her rule.

She shook her head free of such thoughts. It was best to do as Changa asked and focus on the situation before them. There would be more than enough time to deal with other things if they defeated Usenge. If they did not, succession would be the farthest thing from their minds.

Bakomito and Mulunda came to her fire later that night.

"What have you discovered?" she asked.

"They hold the captives in the center of the camp," Mulunda answered. "The white men make up the perimeter. They have guards watching during the night, although they are not very attentive."

"We were able to slip into the camp to the captives," Bakomito said. "We told them to be ready."

"Good," Vatukemba said. "Get some rest."

"Yes, Mama," they said in unison.

Vatukemba sharpened her short sword as the scouts left her fire.

"I will do my part Changa," she said aloud. "Now you must do yours."

* * *

When Johan awoke it was still dark. Usually a heavy sleeper, this journey had put him on edge. Everything was going along as plan, which bothered him most. He strapped on his sword then marched out to inspect the perimeter. As he expected, the night watch was fast asleep. He approached the first man then kicked him in his rump. The man jumped up, his face twisted in rage.

"Goddamn you! What the…"

The man recognized Joham then his anger faded. "I'm sorry señor," he said. "I just dozed off."

"Sure," Johan said. "That will cost you. Now get up and do your job."

The man picked up his arquebus then stood at attention.

Johan made his way to the second man who stirred as he approached.

"Sorry sir," he said. "I was just…"

"I know," Johan said. "Just take your post."

"Yes…"

There was a cracking sound and the man fell to the ground. Johan immediately crouched as an object whizzed by his head. It struck a nearby tree then tumbled to the ground. It was a war club, the blunt end bristling with teeth.

"To arms! To arms!" he shouted.

The attackers rushed into the camp from every direction. Johan had no time to raise his gun so he unsheathed his sword as he backed into the camp. His men stood and fell to the same fate of the guard, battered by clubs thrown with amazing force and accuracy. He heard a sharp cry then turned; a person covered in leopard skin set upon him with a club and short sword. Johan knocked the sword aside the drove his blade into the man. As he pulled his blade free he heard a roar voiced behind him. He turned to see a terrible sight. Someone had set the captives free and they were attacking his men with whatever they could find. This battle was lost before it began. The only thing he could do was run.

He dashed for the trail, dodging flying clubs. A few of his men had come to the same conclusion and were running as well. Among them was Alfonso, his face flush with anger. This was not the time to hash out differences. They had to escape.

* * *

Vatukemba, Kifunji and Mpata waited in the bush, throwing clubs in their hands. Their prey emerged and they readied themselves. They counted ten in all. It was more than they expected, but that did not deter them. Their clubs would even the odds.

When the men were in range they jumped into the trail and threw their clubs. Three men fell, their skulls cracked. They managed to throw again, sending two more men to their deaths and one falling into the bush with a broken arm. Vatukemba pulled her sword, rushing toward the one she assumed was their leader, the white man with the black beard and wide hat. Before she could reach him, another man leaped before him. The man grinned as he extracted his sword then attacked. Vatukemba evaded his stabs and cuts, keeping her sword close to her side. He was quick and skilled, but he's never faced a Leopard, let alone the Mama. Frustration twisted his face as she continued to avoid his attack. He finally yelled then pulled what looked like a club from his waist belt. He pointed the object at Vatukemba; there was a loud sound and smoke as she twisted away. Something hard and hot grazed her cheek and sent her spinning. She landed on her back in a daze. When the smoke cleared the man stood over her scowling.

As he raised his sword Vatukemba swept his feet from under him. She lifted her sword as he fell forward, impaling himself on the blade. Vatukemba pushed the man off, pulling he sword from his convulsing body as she clamored to her feet. She rushed to join the melee.

* * *

Joham watched in terror as Alfonso fell onto the wild woman's sword. He stumbled backwards as his men were decimated. There was nothing left for him to do but save himself. If he was lucky he could return to Usenge and beg his favor. He could not sail a ship back to Portugal alone.

He turned to run but found his way blocked by another wild woman. This woman was smaller than the one who killed Alfonso, but the way she held her war clubs spoke of her experience. Joham took out his dagger then attacked. The woman blocked his attack deftly, dodging the thrusts she could not deflect. Johan pressed harder, using his size to his advantage. The woman's defense faltered; Joham grinned as his sword punctured her torso. He expected the woman to fall, instead she spun away. Her club grazed his head, the teeth cutting a gash across his forehead. Blood poured in his eyes, blinding him. Pain flashed his head and he fell to his knees. He flailed about with his sword and dagger in desperation.

"Where are you bitch? Where are you?"

The top of his head caved in and Joham was swallowed by pain and darkness.

* * *

Vatukemba searched for the man who led them and found him at Kifunji's feet, his head bashed in. Kifunji's hands pressed against her stomach, blood seeping through her fingers. She smiled at Vatukemba then her eyes rolled back before she collapsed. Vatukemba rushed to her. She wrapped her arms around Kifunji, lifting her from the ground. She held her tight until she stopped breathing, then lay her gently on the ground. When she looked up her children and the others surrounded her.

"Back to the camp," she said. "We'll gather the others. Once we know the captives are safe we'll go to Alongi. We're done here."

"I will see to Kifunji and stay with the others," Mpata said. "You go. Changa needs you."

Vatukemba stood as her daughter took her place beside Kifunji. She looked at the others, her stern countenance returning.

"Come," she said.

Her Leopard Children gathered their clubs then sprinted with her into the darkness.

- 18 -

Changa knew it would be impossible taking Usenge by surprise but still he hoped. His scouts, those who managed to return unseen, brought the news he expected. Alongi was prepared for their attack. Palisades surrounded the perimeter with ranks of spearmen behind them. Tukuju lurked the city streets while others waited in ambush inside homes. Those who were not fighting had been evacuated from the city and were being held in camps nearby to prevent escape. In the city center Usenge and his elite Tukuju waited. Changa felt the ancestors' blessing surging though his body, but he knew the reality. Though he was stronger than he'd ever been, he wasn't immortal. Many warriors would die the longer it took him to get to Usenge. The real battle that would determine the fate of the Kongo was between them.

The woods surrounding the city had been cleared. They would have to attack across open field, exposing them to archers. Changa had anticipated as much and prepared his warriors accordingly. Each warrior carried a large wooden shield reinforced with metal strips. The warriors were not happy with the added weight, preferring melee battle to organized assault. But as Changa told them, they would have to be alive to gain their honor, and if they did not carry the shields they'd be so full of poison from the arrows the buzzards and jackals wouldn't eat them.

A rumble from the distance caught his attention. He looked to the east and spotted a vanguard of dark clouds approaching. Lighting flashed between them; moments later the voice of the storm reached his ears.

"The rains come early," Ligongo said.

"This is not seasonal rain," Changa replied. "This is Usenge's doing."

"Is he that powerful?"

"Apparently so," Changa said. "The rain won't work in either of our favor. It's what the rains bring within them that worry me. I remember a similar cloud in the moments before Usenge attacked Cilombo."

Ligongo's face expressed his uneasiness.

Changa waved his hand dismissively.

"There is nothing more we can do," he said. "It is in the ancestors' hands. Let's finish this."

He stepped into the clearing, shield braced on his left arm, throwing knife in his right hand. The other leaders emerged behind him, ranks of warriors following. Changa beat a slow rhythm on his shield and the other leaders followed his pace. The warriors marched forward with the rhythm. The pace was meant to keep them in formation. They had to be close to protect themselves from a possible arrow shower. Any warrior caught alone would be quickly overwhelmed by the poison deluge. The rainstorm edged closer; Changa felt a raindrop on his cheek then braced for the coming downpour. It came moments later, announced by a bright lightning flash and deafening crack of thunder. The sound reverberated across the clearing; it was answered by a roar from Usenge's palisades. A nauseous pang gripped Changa's stomach as a feeling just as jolting filled his mind.

"No!" he said.

A swarm of tebos hurdled the palisades in their various wretched forms, running toward the warriors. Amidst all the challenges and preparations, Changa had forgotten his constant hunters. Only he held the means of defeating them and there were too many. His leaders responded to the unexpected attack, waving their arms and pointing to the bush. The warrior ranks broke down as they dropped their shields and fled. Changa did not run. He could not defeat them all, but he would have to try. He prayed the ancestors granted him the strength to do so.

A flash of lightning blinded him as it struck the ground before him. Changa was thrown on his back but quickly recovered, picking up his shield and knife. Dense smoke blocked his view of the tebo attack and his shifted nervously, not knowing from which direction the beasts would emerge from the obstruction. He stepped back as the smoke shifted as if alive.

"What further madness is this?" he asked aloud.

The smoke continued to swirl, meshing itself into two towering human-like figures. Changa's consternation turned to joy as the facial features of the beings became obvious. One had once been a powerful ally; the other a dangerous adversary. They stood before him, their expressions telling him all he needed to know. Despite the approaching horde he prostrated before them.

"Kintu. Bahati. Your help is most welcomed."

Kintu grinned down. The warrior was bare-chested, a horned helmet atop his head. A massive leaf shield strapped to his left arm. He held a mace the size of a small tree in his right.

"The ancestors favor you," Kintu said.

Changa looked at Bahati. The woman's beauty almost made him forget the dire situation before him. Bahati's body was covered with leather armor. She wore no helmet, her hair a black halo. She held a short stabbing spear in her left hand and a curved sword in her right.

"The ancestors are forgiving," she said. "We share clear a path for you."

Kintu and Bahati charged into the midst of the tebos, Kintu smashing the beasts with shield and mace, Bahati spearing and slicing them with spear and sword. They herded the mindless beasts apart with their fierce onslaught, clearing a way to Usenge's barricades as promised. Changa was spellbound by their fury, his mind distracted from his purpose.

"What are you waiting for, baKongo?" Kintu yelled.

Changa turned toward the woods.

"What are you waiting for?" he shouted to his men.

He waved his arms to his cohorts and they immediately responded. The ranks reformed and the warriors marched forward, many of them cutting their eyes at the supernatural battles taking place on either side of them.

"Eyes forward!" Ligongo shouted.

They were yards away from the barricade when the arrows came. Changa ran backwards, joining the ranks directly behind him. He locked his shield with the others and the arrows riddled the wood. As he expected the spear throwers attempted to take advantage of their position, throwing their spears at their exposed torsos. The front ranks quickly lowered their shields, blocking most of the spears. Some found their marks; warriors tumbled to the ground, some mortally wounded, others less so. The ngangas among them dragged the wounded away and immediately administered antidotes while patching wounds. The others continued forward, covered by their shields.

They reached the barricades.

"Shield down!" Changa and the other commanders shouted.

The warriors at the vanguard piled their shield against the barricades, forming angled platforms that reached the top of the walls. The warriors in the rear rushed up the platforms then plunged down on the surprised warriors. Changa rushed over, throwing knives in both hands. Usenge's warriors fell back, attempting to reorganize. While Changa's warriors swarmed into the city, Changa sprinted toward its center. Usenge waited, and he would not disappoint him.

Tukujus waited as well. The first to jump in his path fell victim to a throwing knife which impaled its head. The second Tukuju died the same. Changa collected his knives and pressed forward. The Tukuju continued their ambushes and Changa continued to kill them, never losing his stride. As the road grew wider, the Tukuju became more organized. They attacked him in pairs and trios, forcing Changa to abandon his knives and use his sword and dagger. He became a blur of death, blocking, slashing and stabbing his way through the Tukuju that swarmed around him like relentless hornets. Changa did not tire, nor did his foes, relenting only when he had shredded them beyond function. The war cries of hundreds of voices reached his ears as his warriors had finally fought their way through the perimeter and joined him in his battle against the half-dead. They did not fare as well as he did yet they fought with fury. They beat a path through Usenge's minions, open a way for Changa. He hesitated; his men needed him. He was turning back when Ligongo appeared, his body covered with blood and tebo ichor.

"Go," he shouted. "Finish this!"

Changa continued his sprint toward the center. For a moment he ran alone through the empty streets then a sharp roar caught his ear. He looked to either side of him then grinned; the Leopards had returned. Vatukemba jumped before him, flanked by her children. They cleared the way of any warrior brave enough to attack, taking them down with their throwing clubs. With their help Changa reached the center of Usenge's stronghold unscathed.

A rank of Tukuju stood before them, blocking the way to Usenge's palace. They charged the Leopard warriors and were met with a barrage of clubs that battered and diminished their ranks. The two groups clashed, Vatukemba leading the way with a piercing cry. Changa waded into the fray, slashing and stabbing with his throwing knives. The fierce Tukuju fell before him like ripe sorghum to a sharp scythe. He had only one thought in his mind; finding and defeating Usenge.

As they disposed of the last of the Tukuju the wet ground vibrated under their feet. Changa's eyes were drawn to Usenge's palace. The building quaked, its thatch roof rippling like the surface of a stormy sea.

"Down!" Changa shouted.

He dove for the mud as the palace exploded. Most of the Leopards avoided the flying wood and stone, some were knocked unconscious or killed by the debris. A deafening roar followed the blast, pulling Changa and the others back to their feet. As the dust and debris settled, Usenge emerged, his hands gripped around the hilt of the beheading sword. This was not the sorcerer Changa faced earlier. He loomed larger, his muscles barely contained by his black skin. His face was still hidden by the mask, his eyes burning red though its eye slits.

"You have returned, Son of Mfumu," he said. "You think your ancestors will save you. But you are not the only one who has gained favor!"

Usenge threw his head back and yelled. His body grew larger as course black hair sprouted from his skin. His mask shattered as he lowered his head. Changa scowled, twisting his knives in his hands as Usenge reached full transformation. An Ndoki stood before him, a sorcerer encased in the body of a silverback, a form as strong physically as the nyama the sorcerer possessed. Usenge pounded the ground with his left hand as he waved the sword in his right.

Vatukemba and her warriors braced themselves despite the fear in their eyes. Changa pushed through them then touched Vatukemba's shoulder.

"Get to a safe place," he said. "This is not your fight."

"You cannot defeat this thing alone!" she replied.

Changa smiled. "I can. I have before. Run!"

The Leopards needed no more urging. They fled in every direction except toward the hulking man-beast before them. Usenge loped toward Changa, the sword that killed his father waving in his right hand. Changa ran as well, his throwing knives at guard. Usenge cleaved down at Changa who spun away as he slashed at Usenge's torso. He smiled as the sorcerer cried out, the knife blades cutting through his hairy skin. Changa's celebration was short-lived; Usenge's left palm slammed into his chest and sent him tumbling into the mud.

Changa held onto his knives then regained his feet. Usenge approached him again but this time more cautiously. Blood ran from his wounds and he grimaced as he pounded toward Changa. Changa's chest throbbed from Usenge's blow but he ignored the pain, focusing on his supernatural foe.

Usenge attacked again. His beastly form was powerful and quick, testing all of Changa's abilities. Changa blocked and dodged the flailing sword, inflicting damage whenever he could. Through the furious exchange he noticed a difference in his opponent. Each cut he inflicted seemed to diminish Usenge's stature and fury. Unfortunately, Usenge's blade had the same effect on him.

Changa blocked a swing meant for his neck and the throwing knife flew from his weakened grip. He dueled Usenge with a solitary knife, his hands shaking as he protected himself from Usenge's powerful blows. As he side-stepped another cut, he struck out with his fist in frustration. He landed the punch in Usenge's ribs and the sorcerer cried out louder than when he was cut by the blade. Changa smiled. He was never meant to defeat Usenge with his knives.

He threw his other knife away. Usenge stopped then laughed.

"You fool!" he exclaimed.

Changa said nothing as he shuffled from side to side, taking the traditional fighting stance of his people. Usenge charged, his sword pulled back to deliver a killing blow. The sorcerer swung and Changa did not move. Instead he caught Usenge's wrist with both hands then twisted his arms and body, flipping the man-beast onto his back. He wrenched the sword from Usenge's hand then flung it away. Usenge yanked his hand free then rolled away, coming to his feet a distance from Changa.

"You think you can defeat me like this? Look at me! I'll crush your frail frame!"

Usenge's attack was vicious, but he could not match Changa's speed and dexterity. Changa landed quick kicks and quicker punches, each blow taking the sorcerer's strength away. Usenge's torso was bruised, his face swelling. He attempted to run for his sword but Changa swept his feet from under him. Man and man-beast struggled in the mud until Usenge wrapped his massive arms around Changa's torso then struggled to his feet. Changa managed to lift his arms free of Usenge's grip then slammed his hands on Usenge's thick neck, squeezing with all his might. For a moment both were locked in a morbid embrace, Changa choking Usenge as the Ndoki pressed the breath from his lungs.

Usenge's determined visage degraded into panic as Changa's finger dug into his weakening throat. His eyes bulged as he fell to one knee then to the other. Changa's squeezed tighter; Usenge released Changa then pried at his hands. Changa pushed the diminished beast onto his back, his grip relentless. Usenge thrashed in the mud in a final attempt to throw Changa free, but Changa locked his legs about Usenge's torso, refusing to be tossed away. The Ndoki finally went limp, his desperate eyes losing all signs of resistance. Changa continued to squeeze as he glared into the sorcerer's black orbs.

"No," Changa said. "You will not die so easy."

Changa released his grip then trudged away, searching through the pouring rain. He finally found what he was seeking; Usenge's execution sword. He lifted the heavy blade and the image of his baba kneeling before Usenge flashed in his mind. For all his life the scene of that day sparked helplessness and fear inside him, but not this day. As he staggered back Usenge rolled onto his belly then struggled onto his knees and hands. He turned his shaggy head toward Changa. A smile came to his face.

"You are truly the Son of Mfumu," he rasped.

Changa leaped the distance between them, the sword raised over his shoulder. He swung with all the strength left in him. The blade sliced through Usenge's neck then sank into the mud. The sorcerer's head fell away as his body collapsed. Changa yanked the sword from the ground. There was no feeling of triumph or satisfaction, only a small sense of vindication and justice. Pain and fatigue seeped into his body and he swayed. His dropped the sword, no longer able to hold it. The world around him darkened, the sound of the rain diminishing into silence. He fell backwards, overwhelmed by a sense of peace as he struck the mud.

For a time, there was stillness and silence. Gradually his senses returned to him. Someone was holding him, their comforting arms and hands bringing warmth to his damaged body. His ears finally accepted the sounds of mourning surrounding him, the wailing and cries like a bright light in his head. He opened his eyes to see a face he had not seen since he was eight years old, a face that was contorted in despair then as it was now.

"Mama," he whispered.

Changa watched mama's expression change from grief, to astonishment to joy. She screamed and two other faces pressed against hers, faces he recognized despite the passage of time. Balela and Malu cried as well, blissful tears meshing with the raindrops on their faces. They crowded around him, their arms competing with mama to hold him.

"He's alive," someone shouted. "Changa is alive!"

A roar like benevolent thunder carried over the city. Changa struggled to sit up and the warriors danced about despite just ending the most important battle of their lives. Drumming reached Changa's ears and the celebration matched pace with it. He lifted his arms and tried his best to hug his family at once.

Silence fell over them. Changa saw awe in his mama's face as she peered over his shoulder. He twisted about and jumped to his feet, expecting the worst. Instead he looked into the smiling faces of Kintu and Bahati. Both were covered in tebo blood and gore, but to Changa they looked immaculate.

"Thank you," Changa said. "Without you we could not have succeeded."

Kintu shook his head.

"The real battle was between you and Usenge," he said. "Nothing else mattered. Our presence was to make sure it came to pass."

Kintu took a knee before Changa then placed his hand on Changa's shoulder.

"You carried me inside you until you no longer needed me," Kintu said. "The ancestors chose you long ago. It took time for you to believe what they always knew."

The demi-god stood as Bahati came to his side.

"There is one more thing I must do for you," Kintu said.

Changa looked with puzzlement at the demi-god. "What is it?"

Kintu grinned. "Do not worry, Son of Mfumu. It is but a little thing. When it is done you will know."

The sky darkened over them all. Kintu and Bahati held each other close.

"Live well, Son of Mfumu," Bahati said. "We will be waiting."

The rain increased into a torrent, obscuring both celestial warriors. As it receded they faded away until they were no more. The clouds parted, the light of dusk illuminating the scene. Many had died, but many more survived. Changa turned to see his mama and sisters gazing at him in wonder. Vatukemba, Ligongo and his other commanders stood behind them, admiration clear on their weary faces. Changa had often dreamed of this moment and now it was here. There was satisfaction, yet he knew this was not the end of his safari. There was one more thing to do.

Changa pushed his way through the celebrating warriors until he found Usenge's body. The sorcerer looked frailer in death, his shriveled body hunched close to his head. Changa took the thin gold band from his head, the band that was the symbol of kabaka for his people. He gazed upon it for a moment; such a small object symbolized so much power. His commanders surrounded him looking upon him expectantly. Changa held

the crown ring up for a few more moments. A smirk
came to his face as he walked to his commanders then
placed the crown of Kongo on Vatukemba's head.

"What? No!" she exclaimed. She tried to take the
band from her head but Changa pushed her hands away.

"The ancestors chose you, not me," she said.

Changa smiled. "The ancestors told me I was
worthy of defeating Usenge. They did not tell me I was
destined to rule Kongo. That is your task and your burden."

Vatukemba eyes darted among the other commanders.

"But...I left Kongo," she said.

"Yes, you did, and you formed a realm of your
own while continuing the fight against Usenge when you
could. If anyone has proven themselves to rule the ba-
Kongo, it is you."

Changa grasped Vatukemba's hand then turned
toward his commanders and the others.

"The ancestors did not tell me that Vatukemba
should be your kabaka," he said. "I know that many of
you might resent her, but you cannot deny her leader-
ship, her strength and her bravery. For many years you
waited for my return. When I finally came, you followed
me not knowing if I could truly fulfill your expectations.
I ask that you trust me one last time and accept Vatukemba as your kabaka."

The commanders exchanged glances. Other leaders emerged from the ranks, chiefs of small villages and
head merchants. They mumbled among themselves as
they looked at Changa and Vatukemba. Finally, Ligongo
came forward.

"I will speak for the others," he said. "It is true
that we are not fond of Vatukemba, but our feelings toward her have nothing to do with her actions against us.
She left us at a time when we thought we needed every

warrior to defeat Usenge. The truth is that even if she had remained the results would not have changed. Vatukemba is no guiltier than any of us."

Ligongo stepped forward then halted before Vatukemba.

"Changa has defeated Usenge. His word had weight. If the ancestors agree with him, you will be our kabaka."

Ligongo prostrated before Vatukemba and the other leaders repeated the gesture. As the sky cleared to the dusk the others prostrated as well. When it was done, only Vatukemba, Changa and his family still stood.

"Are you sure of this, Changa?" Vatukemba asked.

"I am."

Vatukemba chuckled. "Kifunji would have been disappointed. She planned on being a kabaka's wife."

"Would have?" It took Changa a moment to understand.

"I'm sorry," he finally said.

Vatukemba nodded. "She died as a Leopard should. There is no sorrow for her, only joy."

As the others stood Changa made his way to his mother and sisters.

"The war is over," he said. "I leave the details to you."

"And what will you do, Son of Mfumu?" Vatukemba asked.

Changa looked at his mother and sisters.

"I will be a son and a brother," he replied.

He staggered away with his family's help, then disappeared inside the former home of Usenge.

The brave ones had been buried, their souls mourned by their loved ones. The wounded were cared for, but what they had experienced over the many years of Usenge's reign could never be erased. Though many of the warriors had returned to their home villages and cities, many remained to hunt down and kill the remnants of Usenge's hordes. While Kongo worked to bring the world back to normal, Changa spent his time getting to know his family again. Vatukemba assigned them a host of servants to tend to their needs as they shared time with each other. His sisters wished to roam the city and the surroundings, happy to be free of Usenge's yoke. His mother, however, remained close to the home. She insisted Changa stay nearby, asking him over and over again to tell her of his travels and exploits. On one particular evening they were all together, sitting under the branches of the ancestor tree. Changa and his sisters sang a song they used to sing as children, mama smiling with a joyful smile on her face. When they finished the song she sat among them, hugging them as tight as her arms allowed. She gave Changa her longest hug. Soon after her mood shifted from easy to serious.

"I see it is time for me to be the stern mama," she said. "For it seems you have not told me everything."

Despite not seeing her for over twenty years, Changa was becoming exasperated.

"Mama, there is nothing left to tell you," he said.

"What about Panya?" she asked.

"I've told you," he said. "She's a special woman. Very special."

"Yet you sit here with me and your sisters," Mama said.

Changa was confused. "Where else would I be?"

"With her?" Mama answered.

Changa fell silent. He could not deny he missed Panya, but he was where he needed to be. There were some things more important than love.

"There is no reason for you to be here," mama said. "You have killed Usenge. You have freed me and your sisters. You have avenged Mfumu."

"But this is my home!" Changa said.

"Kongo was your home," mama replied. "You have traveled to lands most baKongo cannot dream to see. You have fought monsters most could never imagine, and you have defied the most powerful sorcerer of this land. And now a woman who loves you waits, wondering if you are alive or dead, wondering if she will ever see you again. If it was me, I would want my man to return, even if only to let me know he is safe."

"But mama, don't you want me to stay?" Changa asked.

"Of course, I do," she answered. "It was my dream to watch you grow into a strong warrior as you are now, to see you marry and have many children that I would dote over. It was my dream for all of you to have large families with many girls that would bear my name. But that dream was shattered the day Usenge killed your baba."

Changa looked at his sisters and they looked away. They were still young enough to marry and bear children, but would they after all they'd experienced?

"So, you want me to leave," Changa stated.

"No," mama said. "I want you to do what is best for you. I want you to do what will make you happy. Do not stay for me or your sisters. We will all miss you, but after all you've been through, after all we've been through, it's important that we spend the rest of our lives doing that which will bring us the most joy."

Sleep did not come easy for Changa that night nor the following nights. Mama's words and images of

Panya swirled in his head, competing with what he felt was his duty. During the day he distracted himself by helping the men repair the homes of the city. At night his restless bed waited. After a week of uncertainty, his mind settled. Changa knew what he had to do.

He found Vatukemba in her newly constructed palace, issuing the tasks of the day to her court. Changa entered the entrance and everyone fell silent then prostrated before him. Everyone except Vatukemba. She approached him and they nodded.

"It's good to see you Changa," Vatukemba. "I thought we had lost you to your family."

"You did," Changa said. "I need your help."

Vatukemba's smile faded. "What do you wish, Son of Mfumu?"

"I need to borrow your blacksmith for a time," he said. "There are tools that I need which must be made. Then I need to take a few of your woodcutters."

"Whatever you wish," Vatukemba said.

"Thank you, kabaka," Changa said.

Changa turned and began walking away.

"Wait," Vatukemba called out. Changa halted.

"Why do you need these tools and these men?"

Changa looked over his shoulder then smirked.

"I'm going to build a dhow."

- 19 -

Silence reigned over the Deep Forest, a stillness that it had not seen in millennia. The creatures inhabiting the dense darkness were unlike any ever seen or ever imagined. Some had once roamed a different Earth, masters of a realm that existed only in their genetic memories. Others were foul deformations of creatures that would be familiar to the baKongo, beasts that had been twisted by sorcerers attempting to master powers they barely understood. Normally these creatures moved about the dim world constantly, living, fighting dying and being reborn in a cycle untouched by humans. Except this day.

The Ndoki sat in silence in their cave, their minds occupied with the event that occurred weeks ago, the death of Usenge. When they first captured him wandering in their woods, they had meant to give him to the spirits. But they sensed strength inside him that they wished to exploit. They saw him as a stepping stone to something and someone far greater. But Usenge betrayed them. He killed the person they wished to claim then set himself on a pedestal he did not deserve.

"In the end he was weak," the elder Ndoki said. "Fear ruled him, fear of what came to pass."

"As we knew he would be," the second Ndoki agreed.

The third Ndoki, the youngest of the three, said nothing. It stared into the fire as if reading the flames.

"Why do you not speak?" the elder said.

"Because I will not delude myself," it replied. "Yes, we knew he was weak. Yet we spared his life and initiated him. We must not make the same mistake again."

"What of Vatukemba?" the elder asked. "She seeks power beyond her position. Greed is weakness."

The other Ndoki nodded.

"We will begin the cycle…"

Its words were interrupted by a sudden flash of light overhead. The Ndoki turned their heads in unison to the disturbance just as a bright streak plunged from the light then struck the ground close enough to them that its impact shook them. The Deep Forest awoke with the cries of beasts as the Ndoki stood, their eyes closed. What they sensed brought shock and fear to their faces.

"Summon them all!" the elder shouted. The forests around them seemed to move in unison toward the landfall of the light. The Ndoki move toward it as well. For the first time since any of them could remember, they felt fear.

*   *   *

Kintu emerged from the debris of his landing, his club and shield braced for battle. The woods before him writhed as hordes of creatures approached, sent by their masters to kill him. That was not possible. He crouched then sprang upward, looking down at the situation below. The monsters advanced from every direction, the Ndoki following close behind. They were his target, but their beasts posed a problem as well. Left without the spiritual tethers that kept them subdued they would roam the forests killing everything and everyone in their path. Though he had not planned to do so, he realized he would have to kill them all. He hovered a moment

longer, waiting until the horde bunched about his landfall, their roars and shrieks reaching his ears. Then he
fell like a raptor into their midst. His impact killed the
closest immediately, their carcasses crashing into the
other. Kintu swung his mace and his shield, slicing and
crushing the beasts as they attacked. He crushed the
horde like a grindstone into the harvest, smashing the
beasts in all the directions. Despite their fruitless efforts
they continued to attack, driving by their desperate masters. They were too shallow to know that the thing they
attacked knew nothing of fear or fatigue. Kintu trampled
over a growing pile of dead and dying beasts, his focus
unwavering. He was finishing the last of the demented
herd when a blast of energy streaked in his direction. He
raised his shield, blocking the bolt. The impact knocked
him backwards. A smile came to his face.

"The battle begins," he said.

He lowered his shield. The Ndoki stood before
him, pounding the earth with their wrists and barking
their anger. Kintu could feel their strength, both physical
and spiritual and for a moment wished he had brought
Bahati with him. The sorcerers separated, one to the
right, the other to the left. The largest of the three, a huge
amalgam of silverback and man, remained still, glaring
at the warrior.

"Why have you come here?" it growled. "This is
not your concern!"

Kintu glared back.

"You have angered the ancestors with your interference," Kintu replied. "You have reached far beyond
your grasp."

"Whatever we wish we gain," the elder Ndoki
said. "And now we wish you dead. Kutmewa!"

The Ndoki was answered by a shrill bellow.
Kintu felt the ground shake beneath his sandaled feet
then braced himself for the attack to come. The elder

Ndoki jumped aside, his form replaced by a charging *vi-faru* of a size the warrior had never seen. It did not matter to him. He shouted then ran at the beast, his shield and club held wide. The beast's red eyes narrowed and they came closer, snorting its displeasure. Just before the moment of contact Kintu lowered his head. Helmet crashed into horns and both adversaries stumbled backwards from a force that would have killed most. Kintu regained his footing the shook his head. His helmet had cracked from the blow, the horn missing; he snatched it off head then tossed it aside. Kintu looked ahead and found his missing horn imbedded into the vifaru's head. The beast staggered as it attempted to shake it free. A moan seeped from its mouth then it collapsed. Kintu sauntered to its trembling body then raised his shield. With two hacks he severed the beast's head. He glared at the elder Ndoki as he stepped over the dead beast.

The Ndoki attacked. They came simultaneously, reaching Kintu at the same time. He spun, club and shield extended and the forest demons jumped away to avoid his blows. Kintu leapt toward the smallest of the three, smashing his shield into the man-beast. It staggered back stunned but avoided the club swing meant to crush its head. Before he could strike again the second Ndoki grabbed his arm then twisted him about. Kintu winced as the beast's fist struck his jaw. It had been a long time since he'd been struck with such force. He tasted something bitter in his mouth, it was blood. He smiled, the red fluid seeping between his teeth. The Ndoki over-estimated its damage on the demi-god, raising both hands over its head to strike a killing blow. Kintu jammed his club into the Ndoki's throat then followed with the slash of his shield. The Ndoki's arms and head fell to the ground like over-ripe fruit from a tree, its body following.

Kintu had no time to savor his victory. The smaller Ndoki and the elder man-beast pounded him with fists and feet, enraged by the death of their cohort. He twisted back and forth, blocking the blows that he could and absorbing the others. He felt his body weakening, another sensation he had not experience in centuries. But there was no panic in his face, only resolve. He slowed his pace, allowing the smaller Ndoki to grab his club. As the man-beast yanked it Kintu let the momentum carry him to the beast. The elder Ndoki clamped his hands on Kintu's shoulders but it was too late. The sharp edge of Kintu's shield sank into the small Ndoki's chest, cutting through bone and piercing its heart. He pulled the shield free and the Ndoki collapsed, dead before it reached the ground.

The elder Ndoki's roar filled Kintu ears before it flung him away. The warrior twisted in flight then landed on his feet. He still held his shield, but his club was gone. The elder Ndoki held the club in its hand, its back turned to Kintu. It turned slowly then leveled its eyes on the warrior, bright light blazing in its sockets. It released another roar then crossed the distance between them with incredible alacrity. Kintu raised his shield as the Ndoki beat at him like a maddened drummer, gripping the club with both hands. The hammer dented the shield with each blow, Kintu's body jerking as he protected himself.

"Enough!" Kintu shouted.

He threw his shield aside. The elder Ndoki's eyes shone brighter to match his grin as he brought the club down. But Kintu caught his arms at the wrist. The two struggled, their teeth clenched as the Ndoki struggled to pull his arms free. It jerked with all its might but Kintu's grip held firm. Suddenly Kintu twisted, lifting the Ndoki onto his hip. He continued to twist, slamming the man-beast onto its back. As struck the ground its grip on the club loosened and Kintu snatched the club away. The Ndoki had only a moment to curse its loss before the club smashed into its face again and again until its spirit fled its dying body. Kintu felt the malevolent heat as the spirit passed through him, the elder Ndoki's foul spirit rising to face the judgment of the ancestors.

Kintu stood over the Ndoki's lifeless body for a moment, savoring the quiet his victory instilled over the Deep Forest. He sauntered to his shield then inspected it. It would take The Blacksmith much work to repair it, but the being needed the distraction. He ambled to the Ndoki's body then severed its head with the shield. It was an unnecessary gesture but he did it anyway, succumbing for a moment to his human half. He scanned the battlefield on last time searching for signs of lie. There were none.

"It is done," he said.

Kintu raised his club high. Dark clouds formed over him as he closed his eyes. A huge lightning bolt struck him, its voice following with a force that shook those trees which still stood. Kintu dissipated within the ancestral energy, returning to the ancestors and Bahati.

-20-

Panya fidgeted on her stool as she presided over another boring meeting, her beaded crown hiding her bored expression. The Hausa merchant standing before her showered her with platitudes that went on far too long before finally getting to the reason for his approaching the stool. Tula stood beside her, attentive as always. In the beginning Panya had eagerly taken on the responsibility as Oba of Oyo, but as the months passed she found herself more and more distracted. If asked she would say it was the tedious ceremony that came with the position, but deep inside there was another reason she grew impatient with the responsibility.

The merchant was reaching the climax of his soliloquy when a warrior burst into the royal tent, his chest heaving with exertion. Tula stepped forward, a frown on her child-like face.

"What is the meaning of this?" she said.

"Forgive me, Oba," the warrior said before prostrating before the room full of dignitaries.

"But the dockmaster sent me."

Panya sat up on the stool, her heart beating against her chest.

"And?" Tula asked.

"A ship has arrived…"

Panya gathered her robes in her hand then jumped from the stool, sprinting through the tent and by the startled warrior. She ran through the city, people shouting curses at her as they jumped out of her path until they realized who she was. She was halfway to the beach when her guards caught up with her then ran before her, clearing a path through to throng. As the guards cleared the final person from her path she saw why the dockmaster sent the warrior and her heart raced. A small dhow bobbed on the gentle waves. Pulling the rope attached to its prow was a shirtless man, his powerful muscles rippling as he towed the ship in. The man looked up and Panya felt a rush of joy that almost made her faint.

"Changa!" she screamed.

Changa waded through the surf, pulling the dhow behind him. He heard his name called and he looked toward the gathering crowd. A woman stood surrounded by guards, dressed in the finery of a ruler, holding her robes high. Her face hidden by her beaded crown. The woman snatched the crown from her head then ran toward the surf, a smile on her beautiful and familiar face.

"Panya," he whispered.

Changa let go of the rope then ran to the beach, high-stepping through the waves. As they converged Panya let go of her robes then jumped into his waiting arms. Their kiss was better than he imagined; deep, long and luxurious. Their tears mingled as they continued to kiss, afraid to stop. But stop they did. Panya looked into his eyes in a way that let him know his world was finally complete.

"You came back," she said. "You came back to me."

"Of course I did," Changa replied. "You are my life."

"I wasn't sure you would," she said. "I wasn't sure you would kill Usenge and if you did, I wasn't sure if you would want to leave your family again or if your people would let you."

"Usenge is dead by my hand," Changa said. "My mother and sisters are free, as are the people of Kongo. There is a new leader in Kongo and she will govern them well."

"So, you left your family again," Panya said.

"I will not lie. It was hard. To be away from them for so long and to leave again was not easy. But the longer I stayed the more certain I knew where I needed to be. I am from Kongo, but home is wherever you are."

They kissed again then walked hand in hand to the shore. The others of the court had come to the beach, looks of wonder on their faces. They had reached the shore before Changa realized someone was missing.

"Where is Tula?" he asked.

"I am here."

The crowd parted, revealing Panya's advisor and friend. Walking beside her were a boy and a girl, both holding her hands.

"Welcome home, Changa," Tula said.

Changa nodded, his face puzzled.

"I see much has changed since I left," Changa said. "Are these your children?"

"No," Panya said. "They are ours."

The words struck Changa harder than any blow.

"Ours?"

Tula let go of the children's hands and they ran to Panya.

"Mama! Mama!"

Panya knelt and hugged them both.

"When you left two years ago I knew I was pregnant," Panya said.

Despite his joy Changa felt a hint of anger.

"And you did not tell me?"

"No," Panya said. "If I had you would not have gone."

Changa knelt beside Panya, getting a good look at his children for the first time.

"The ancestors blessed us with twins," Panya said. She pointed at the girl. "This is Taiwo. Our son is Kehinde."

Changa opened his arms. Taiwo came to him immediately. Kehinde grabbed Panya robes and hid his face.

"It's okay Kehinde," Panya said. "This is your baba."

Kehinde uncovered his face then crept toward Changa.

"It's okay," Changa said.

Kehinde finally came to him. Changa gathered them into his arms then stood. Panya came to him and wrapped her arms around his waist.

"I am home," he said. "I am truly home."

"Your safari is over," Panya said.

"Yes, it is," Changa replied.

Together they walked toward the village. The court and the others gathered around them and they disappeared among the throng. No one noticed as the dhow drifted away, carried out to sea by Oya's hand.

-end-

AFTERWORD

Changa's Safari began as an idea over thirty years ago. His creation was inspired by Robert E. Howard's Conan. I wanted to create a character that was similar yet different than the roaming barbarian, a character that would be of African descent and become the type of literary hero I never had as a child. Now, decades later, the Safari has come to an end. I hope you have enjoyed reading Changa's adventures as much as I have enjoyed writing them, and I hope you share them with anyone and everyone you know that loves a grand and exciting adventure.

A special shout out goes to my wife Vickie, who was the first to hear Changa's adventures and has served as my muse and foundation for Changa's friend and eventually love, Panya. Another special shout out goes to my former college English instructor and now friend Anna Holloway, who was the first person to encourage me to take writing seriously and planted the seed of my interest in science fiction and fantasy. And a final shout out to everyone who chose to take a chance on a self-published black writer and join the Safari. Thank you for your patience and your support.

Changa's journey has come to an end. But there is much more to come. Stay tuned.

MILTON J DAVIS

ABOUT THE AUTHOR

Milton Davis is a Black Speculative fiction writer and owner of MVmedia, LLC, a small publishing company specializing in Science Fiction, Fantasy and Sword and Soul. MVmedia's mission is to provide speculative fiction books that represent people of color in a positive manner. Milton is the author of seventeen novels; his most recent is the Sword and Soul adventure *Son of Mfumu*. He is the editor and co-editor of seven anthologies; *The City, Dark Universe* with Gene Peterson; *Griots: A Sword and Soul Anthology and Griot: Sisters of the Spear*, with Charles R. Saunders; *The Ki Khanga Anthology*, the *Steamfunk! Anthology*, and the *Dieselfunk anthology* with Balogun Ojetade. MVmedia has also published *Once Upon A Time in Afrika* by Balogun Ojetade and *Abegoni: First Calling* and *Nyumbani Tales* by Sword and Soul creator and icon Charles R. Saunders. Milton's work had also been featured in *Black Power: The Superhero Anthology*; Skelos *2: The Journal of Weird Fiction and Dark Fantasy Volume 2*,

MILTON J DAVIS

Steampunk Writes Around the World published by Luna Press and *Bass Reeves Frontier Marshal Volume Two.*

Milton resides in Metro Atlanta with his wife Vickie and his children Brandon and Alana.

JUL 0 8 2018

CPSIA information can be obtained
at www.ICGtesting.com
Printed in the USA
LVHW03s2318150618
580966LV00001B/29/P